# Praise for
## *Woodson Falls: 16 Lakeview Terrace*

Against the routine backdrop of a small New England town, Andrea O'Connor successfully weaves a gripping page-turner, ending with a bang. The fictional town, Woodson Falls, is itself an expertly drawn character and O'Connor's knowledge of her terrain is masterful right down to the most obscure zoning ordinance. *Woodson Falls: 16 Lakeview Terrace* is perfect for mystery lovers, and her spirited protagonist, Attorney Gaby Quinn, resonates so strongly that one wonders what other mysteries she might unravel in future novels.

**—Don Lowe, First Selectman, Sherman, CT**

O'Connor gets the pace and detail of small town, rural Connecticut, the land of steady habits, just right, in her first mystery. Her background as a nurse, an attorney, and a hands-on elected official really shines through in her descriptions of local land use policy and probate courts, which she makes easily understandable, all the while cleverly hiding clues among these mundane topics. Yes, small towns almost always have big secrets, and you'll enjoy hunting for them in O'Connor's delightful tale of intrigue in *Woodson Falls: 16 Lakeview Terrace*.

**—Cheryl D. Reedy, former First Selectman, New Fairfield, CT**

There is something warm and cozy about Andrea O'Connor's first Attorney Gaby Quinn mystery, *Woodson Falls: 16 Lakeview Terrace*. A small-town atmosphere is brilliantly created in this intriguing conundrum that has a strong finish that will shock and surprise you. A fine writing style moves the puzzle along in an effortless pace and Ms. O'Connor's lead character, Gaby Quinn, is a pleasure to follow around. *Woodson Falls: 16 Lakeview Terrace* is a good read for anyone who likes a clever mystery.

—**Peter Green, author of the Jimmy Dugan mystery series**

No one knows what to make of Pieter Jorgenson in the small Connecticut town of Woodson Falls. A school crossing guard who's always nice to children, he has few admirers among the town's adults. Sullen and reclusive, he has no friends, and he never allows others into his isolated lakeside home. When he dies suddenly on a trip to New York City, he leaves no will to settle his unexpectedly large estate. A local judge assigns a young attorney, Gabriella Quinn, to handle his affairs. As she delves into the case, she finds herself drawn into the dark landscape of his life; the tension builds as she discovers the shocking truth about him. Andrea O'Connor's novel, *Woodson Falls: 16 Lakeview Terrace*, is a story of mounting intrigue and menace.

—**R.C. Goodwin, author of *Model Child* and *The Stephen Hawking Death Row Fan Club***

Everyone wants a small New England town to be peaceful and predictable with the safety and security not found in the drama of the Big Apple. Attorney Gaby Quin moved to Woodson Falls for that very reason. Unfortunately for Gaby, evil knows no bounds. Author Andrea O'Connor brings you to the lovely New England town of Woodson Falls and takes you down a road no one wants to go.

—**Marc Youngquist, author of the *Maidstone* mysteries**

In this twisted mystery, Andrea O'Connor takes the reader on a journey through real estate law (and makes it interesting) to a very bizarre ending. And, we're not talking run-of-the mill bizarre, but really, really you-don't-see-it-coming bizarre. Excellent read.

—**Robin Taney, Studio 4 PR**

Woodson Falls is a charming town, where folks know one another and willingly help each other. As a retired probate judge, I was delighted to read the factual, clear detailing of estate administration, which had young lawyer Gaby Quinn unearthing information about family trees, lawsuits, town regulations, the decedent's property, and questionable happenings. As Gaby administers the estate of a Woodson Falls resident few people knew, Andrea O'Connor sets up a surprising conclusion subtly hinted at throughout the story. I would have welcomed Gaby Quinn in my court!

— **Judge Barbara J. Ackerman, retired**

# Woodson Falls: 16 Lakeview Terrace

*A Gaby Quinn Mystery*

# Woodson Falls: 16 Lakeview Terrace

*A Gaby Quinn Mystery*

by
Andrea O'Connor

EMERALD LAKE
**BOOKS**
Sherman, Connecticut

Books published by Emerald Lake Books may be ordered through your favorite booksellers or by visiting emeraldlakebooks.com.

Library of Congress Cataloging-in-Publication Data

Names: O'Connor, Andrea B., author.

Title: Woodson Falls : 16 Lakeview Terrace / by Andrea O'Connor.

Description: Sherman, CT : Emerald Lake Books, [2020] | Series: A Gaby Quinn mystery | Summary: "Gaby Quinn is hiding from her past, recovering from the senseless death of her husband, and living in a small New England town. She has her law practice, her dog Kat, and a small circle of friends. What more could she need? But when an unusual probate case crosses her desk, she finds herself looking for a lost body, an abandoned truck, and answers to a mountain of questions, not least of which is, "Who was Pieter Jorgenson?" Soon enough, she discovers even small towns hold big secrets"-- Provided by publisher.

Identifiers: LCCN 2020027804 (print) | LCCN 2020027805 (ebook) | ISBN 9781945847264 (paperback) | ISBN 9781945847295 (epub)

Subjects: GSAFD: Legal stories. | Suspense fiction.

Classification: LCC PS3615.C5843 W66 2020  (print) | LCC PS3615.C5843 (ebook) | DDC 813/.6--dc23

LC record available at https://lccn.loc.gov/2020027804

LC ebook record available at https://lccn.loc.gov/2020027805

*For John:*
*This story is as much yours as it is mine.*

# Prologue

"IT'LL BE GOOD TO BE BACK IN MY OWN BED," RALPH SAID TO his wife, Trudy, as they neared Woodson Falls, the last leg of the long drive back from Florida, where they spent the winter months.

"You sure you don't want to sell this place? Live in the Florida condo full-time?" Trudy asked.

"No way! Too hot in the summer and way too many old people. Besides, I like having our own place here in the country. And the view of the waterfall never ceases to calm me down when I get riled up over something or other."

"The falls and the lake are beautiful."

"I wish you'd reconsider and let us buy that lot next to us. A house there would ruin our view."

"Get over it, Ralph. That may be a lot on paper, but it's not buildable. The health department would never approve it under the new rules."

"If we changed the lot lines, maybe we could put in a swimming pool."

"Not worth the money or the work. We have the lake. Plus, we can swim down in Florida."

"Here we are, honey," Ralph said, turning into Lakeview Terrace. "Home, sweet home."

As they approached their house, Trudy gasped. "What in heavens is that?"

A three-story monstrosity had been planted on the adjacent property, jutting out at an angle that blocked the best part of their once-expansive view of Woodson Lake.

"Oh, Ralph. Now what?" Trudy was in tears as they turned at the end of the road to drive down their new neighbor's driveway that once led solely to their home.

# Chapter 1

## (*Two Years Later*)

"WHAT THE HELL DO YOU THINK YOU'RE DOING?" RALPH LOOMIS shouted as he scuttled up his driveway toward his neighbor's property, the last house on Lakeview Terrace. "Just what the hell do you think you're doing?" he repeated, red-faced, leaning forward, fists on his hips as he neared the retaining wall his neighbor, Pieter Jorgenson, was erecting along the property line.

"Buildin' a wall," Jorgenson replied, remaining on his knees. Not looking up, he carefully spread mortar on top of the second row of cement blocks. A dozen or more blocks were stacked to his left, the mortar bucket kept close to the wall where he was working.

"But you're blocking my driveway! I won't be able to get out," Loomis continued.

"Not my problem," Jorgenson said as he laid three cement blocks onto the mortar, tapping them into alignment. He reached for the trowel, pulled up more mortar, and continued with the third layer of cement blocks. The wall extended the length of the property line.

"Don'tcha realize that every property owner this side of Lakeview Terrace gave his neighbor access to get onto the road? Idiot surveyor drew up the lots with no way of driving up to the damn road.

This... this wall'll make it impossible for me to get in and out of my own driveway!"

"Like I said," Jorgenson responded, standing to face his neighbor, "not my problem." A husky man, Jorgenson was all muscle, close to 250 pounds, and at least six-foot-six, dwarfing Loomis, who stepped back involuntarily.

"But... but," Loomis sputtered.

"See here. Your so-called driveway drains onto my property." He pointed with the trowel. "See that there gully along my foundation? Caused by all the water flowin' down the hill and across your driveway toward the lake. Don't need to be worryin' about no water underminin' my foundation. I'm buildin' this here wall to prevent that." He turned back to his work, slapping more mortar onto the cement blocks to finish the final course.

"You'll hear from my lawyer, damn you," Loomis bellowed, turning to hike back down his driveway to the house. "I'm not putting up with this nonsense. Not for one minute."

"So, sue me," called Jorgenson. "I got every right to protect my property. I checked in Town Hall. You can't be divertin' water onto someone else's land. I got rights here."

"We'll just see about that," Loomis yelled. He went into the house, slamming the door behind him.

"I got rights, you runty bastard," Jorgenson muttered, smashing the last of the cement blocks into place. "I got rights."

With the wall between the two properties finally finished, Jorgenson returned his tools and supplies to the garage across the breezeway and re-entered his house. He needed to cool off after that confrontation with Loomis.

Opening the refrigerator, he grabbed the first of the two beers he allowed himself each day and headed downstairs to the shaded deck that ran alongside the lower level of his house. Easing his weight into the lounge chair in the shady corner of the deck, he put up his legs and popped the top of the can of Budweiser, taking a long draught of the cold brew.

He hated people like that. People who thought everything should go their way. People who took pleasure in pushing other people around.

# Chapter 2

GABRIELLA QUINN GAZED OUT THE PICTURE WINDOW AT THE pond below. Most of its snow cover had melted days ago, but a heavy rain followed by a sudden dip in the temperature had left its surface smooth as glass, reflecting the bare trees that lined the shore. She could glimpse Woodson Lake in the distance and imagined the falls beyond, the tumbling waters suddenly frozen into a sculpture worthy of display in a museum.

Pennsylvania's groundhog had predicted six more weeks of winter. *If you believed such things.* Only two weeks to go until Beaver Pond should begin to melt into itself once again, turning a subtle taupe that surely would signal the start of spring. She had chosen this room for her law office because of the view. The ever-changing pond and active wildlife, even in winter, were a source of delight whenever she glanced up from her desk.

She returned to drafting a particularly tricky clause in the contract she was preparing for the Hansen's, who were selling their house. If acceptable to the buyer, this clause would permit Ann and Paul to stay in the house until June, allowing their young daughter Cyndi to finish out the school year before the family moved to Texas. Real estate law wasn't her favorite, but most small law practices like her own survived on the fees real estate transactions generated for the attorney handling the transfer for either buyer or seller. In a larger practice, a paralegal would handle most of the details surrounding such sales, but Gaby wasn't yet in a position to hire a paralegal, even part-time. The telephone rang, interrupting Gabriella's train of thought.

"Law offices. Gabriella Quinn speaking," she said, smiling to herself at the formality of her announcement given the location of her "offices" in this room in the cottage she'd inherited from her grandfather.

"Gaby, good to hear your voice. Bud Taylor calling. I've got an estate I'm hoping you'll take on."

Hiram Samuel "Bud" Taylor had retired from a large estate planning practice some fifteen years ago, winning the seat as Judge for the Foothills Probate District every four years since with little opposition. A tall, stocky man with steely gray hair, he preferred to be called "Bud" rather than "Judge Taylor," but she still had difficulty with that informality.

"Good afternoon, Your Honor. I think I may be able to squeeze it in," she said with a chuckle. She had opened her law practice in Woodson Falls just over two years ago. Fresh out of law school, she had resigned her tenured position as a professor of philosophy at Columbia University after she passed the bar in both New York and Connecticut. "What have you got?"

"Interesting case. Started with a land dispute up in Woodson Lake Estates. Lakeview Terrace, number sixteen. The defendant, by the name of Pieter Jorgenson, failed to appear when the case came up for hearing. The plaintiff, Ralph Loomis, was awarded a judgment by default against Jorgenson on an adverse possession claim when the defendant didn't show up at the trial. Turned out Jorgenson had died suddenly in New York, an apparent stroke or brain aneurysm according to the death certificate. Just in his fifties too. Loomis can't collect on the judgment or remove the wall blocking his access to his property until there's an estate to file a claim against. Bill Harrison, Loomis' attorney, asked me to appoint someone as administrator.

There are no next of kin according to Bill, at least not in Connecticut, and it's likely Jorgenson didn't leave a will. You're the only attorney in Woodson Falls, and I figured you might be interested."

Gaby appreciated the Judge's occasional referrals. She had introduced herself to the Court once she had set up her office, and Judge Taylor and his clerks had welcomed her warmly. Building a law practice from scratch would have been difficult without such referrals.

"Certainly am interested, Judge, and thank you for thinking of me. Let me see… Today's Wednesday. I can stop by to pick up the death certificate tomorrow. I should be able to file the necessary applications early next week."

"Good, good. Knew I could count on you, Gaby. Well, see you tomorrow—or one of my clerks will. Have a good afternoon."

"Thanks, Judge. You too. Bye now."

Hanging up the phone, Gaby scribbled a few notes on the new case, then leaned back in her chair, gazing once again at the pond. She hated the thought of going up to the Estates. The narrow, winding roads in the massive subdivision were tricky to navigate, and it was easy to get caught in a dead-end, where turning around could quickly turn dangerous on the steep hills. The accumulated snow and likely icing of the roads would just make a difficult situation even more hazardous.

"Come on, Katrina," she called to her German Sheprador, a beautiful Shepherd-Labrador mix she had gotten shortly after she moved to Woodson Falls. "Time for a run."

Gaby did her best thinking while she was outside running or, in the summer months, swimming with Kat out to one of the islands in the middle of Woodson Lake. She and the black and tan dog both loved the outdoors, and the trails around Gaby's cottage in the woods of southern Woodson Falls allowed Katrina to run free of a leash. They headed toward a tree-lined trail that ran just across the road and up a steep hill.

*I'll finish up that contract when I get back.* Then she would map out a plan for gathering the information she'd need to file the necessary paperwork with the probate court, formally opening the Jorgenson estate.

An hour later Gaby was back in her office, warming her hands around a mug of cocoa. She laid aside the completed draft of the Hansen contract to be reviewed tomorrow, then reached into a drawer, pulling out her map of Woodson Falls. She located Woodson Lake Estates, which ran along the lake's northwestern shoreline. It was impossible to determine topography on this map, but when she found the squiggly line representing Lakeview Terrace, she suspected it would run along a high ridge. The line drifted off into empty space, one of the many dead-end roads located in most Woodson Falls subdivisions. Hopefully, the house would be one of the first on the road and not the last.

# Chapter 3

GABY'S DOG WAS WAITING AT THE DOOR, TAIL WAGGING, WHILE Gaby gathered her briefcase and purse in preparation for her trip into town. "You should be all tired out, Kat. We had a long run around Deer Pond this morning," she said, scratching the dog's forehead. "You'll have to stay home while I'm out."

The dog turned toward the sofa, then looked back with such mournful eyes that Gaby felt a bit guilty as she slipped out the front door and down the flagstone walk to her car. She knew Kat would be watching from the window for her return, jumping up to greet her as soon as she opened the door, all forgiven. Waving to Kat as she entered her weathered Subaru, Gaby drove down the dirt road fronting her cottage. She turned left onto Pine Hill Road, which eventually connected with Route 41, taking her toward the town center.

Nestled in the foothills of the Berkshires, Woodson Falls lies just east of the ridge of hills marking the western border of Connecticut and New York State. Once a thriving farming community, the town's many dairy farms disappeared over the years in the press for residential development. Now, two-story Colonials set upon two-acre lots dotted the land in place of grazing cattle. The few remaining farms, much reduced in acreage, give witness to Woodson Falls' agricultural heritage but contribute little to its economy.

The full-time resident population hovered at about 2,000 but swelled to nearly 3,500 on weekends and during the summer. However, the main "economic engine" of the town is 82-acre Woodson Lake. The state park along a portion of the shoreline invites residents and visitors alike to enjoy the lake's quiet waters for fishing, swimming and other water sports. No motorboats are permitted on the lake, making it an ideal venue for those who prefer sailing, kayaking, canoing or just sitting to take in the vista, particularly the spectacular waterfall that flows from the northern border of the lake and gives the town its name.

Gaby had spent many happy weeks here with her older sister, Marcia, staying with Grandpa during the summer while their parents attended conferences or did research. She had been surprised when her grandfather bequeathed the cottage to her, along with a hefty sum of money. Owning a place filled with memories of good times spent with Marcia and their grandfather just stirred up unresolved guilt. She had been too wrapped up in her busy life as a junior at Columbia to head home to Middletown before Marcia died of meningitis.

After Gaby married Joe, their lives seldom included a trip to the Connecticut countryside. Even when they did get up to Woodson Falls, the quiet pace of the town made them both impatient to return to the sparkle of life in New York City as a young married couple deeply in love.

Gaby fingered the scar that ran from her temple and around the curve of her left cheek, stopping just short of her mouth. *Don't go there*, she thought with a shake of her head, blinking back the tears that threatened to flow whenever she remembered that dreadful night. When she and Joe were attacked while walking back to their apartment after dinner. When Joe had been knifed and died in her arms, her tears mingling with the blood flowing from her own wounded face.

*Enough!*

As Gaby came to the town center and parked the car, she mentally reviewed her plan to use the day to gather information from Town Hall for the Jorgenson estate, check out the house on Lakeview Terrace, and then head over to Prescott to pick up the death certificate from the probate court. But first, she wanted to stop at Mike's Place, the local market. She had delayed her trip into town until the commuters and tradesmen had departed for work, hoping she could grab a Danish and coffee, and maybe chat with Mike's wife, Emma, who usually manned the deli.

"I was thinking you might stop in today. It seems so long since I last saw you. Saved this for you, just in case," said Emma, handing her a raspberry Danish, Gaby's favorite.

"Great! How ever did you know I'd come by today?" Gaby asked as she brought her coffee and Danish to the area set off to the left of the deli counter, where a few tables and chairs gave customers a place to sit and read the newspaper or talk with a friend over a cup of coffee. "Have time to chat?"

"Sure do, and it'd be a relief to get off my feet for a bit. This morning was really hectic," replied Emma as she plunked down next to her friend. "Then again, most mornings around here are," she added with a smile.

Gaby bit into the Danish, rolling her eyes in enjoyment. "I'm in heaven! Thanks so much for saving this for me." She and Emma continued to talk quietly while Gaby sipped on her coffee and finished the Danish, an occasional laugh punctuating their conversation.

Looking at her watch, Gaby said, "Gotta get going. Ask you a question?"

"Sure. What's up?" The short, energetic blonde loved to gossip, always eager to gather and share information.

"Know anything about a guy named Jorgenson from up in the Estates?"

"Tall, husky guy? Haven't seen him around lately, but he's always polite when he comes in. Buys a sandwich, a six-pack of Bud and picks up a few of those one-gallon plastic bottles of water. Every time. Why?"

"Apparently he died while in New York. Judge Taylor asked me to handle the estate. I'm heading up to the house after I check some stuff in Town Hall."

"Oh, my goodness! He died? What happened?"

"Not quite sure yet."

They both stood as Frank Pastore, owner of the hardware store next door, approached the deli counter.

"Did I overhear you two talking about Pieter Jorgenson?" he asked. "I've been trying to get in touch with him. I'm plum out of those birdhouses he makes. They're a real hit with customers, especially the out-of-towners."

"Afraid you're out of luck, Mr. Pastore," Emma broke in. "Gaby just told me he died in New York."

"Oh, heavens! Hadn't heard." Turning to Gaby, he said, "Let me know about any arrangements, would you?"

"Sure will," Gaby answered. "Catch you later," she called to Emma as she made her way toward the cash register, where Mrs. Browning waited behind the counter. The widow of a retired state trooper, the portly, grey-haired woman was born and raised in Woodson Falls, making her a great source of local historical lore.

"How you doin', Gaby?" she said as she rang up Gaby's purchases.

"Just fine, Betty. Yourself?"

"Can't complain. Nobody'd listen anyway," she replied with a smile.

"Before I leave, can you tell me anything about Pieter Jorgenson? Emma said he shopped here."

"Nice guy. Works as a crossing guard at Woodson Falls Elementary. Kids like him. Call him 'Mr. J.' Probably because he gives some of them snack packs of animal crackers," she said, chuckling. "Orders them from Mike by the case."

"Hmm… Interesting. Thanks for the information. Enjoy the day."

Gaby went to her car, tossing in the bag of treats she had picked up for Kat and pulling out her briefcase. As she was closing the door, she saw Frank Pastore leaving Mike's with a large cup of coffee. "Talk to you for a minute, Frank?" she called.

"Sure. Come on in," he said, opening the hardware store door and waving her inside. He put his coffee down on the counter and donned the work apron he always wore in the shop before picking up the coffee again, sipping it through the plastic cover.

Just a bit taller than Gaby, the wiry shop owner was a trove of information for the do-it-yourselfer. He knew where every bolt and screw was located in his packed store, as well as how to use them. "What can I do for you?"

"I was appointed by the court to handle Pieter Jorgenson's estate, but I never met him and don't know anything about him. I was wondering if you could give me a feel for the man. Anything would help."

"Well, he was a skilled carpenter. Knew his materials and how to use them. He did all the framing and finish work on his house up in the Estates. Just hired a contractor for the foundation work. I pointed him in the direction of a good plumber and electrician as well as who he might contact for the heating system, septic and well. Said he bought the property to build a place in the country for his ailing mother. He hoped the clean air would help her heal.

"I went up there with him once. Told me he had a problem with road drainage and was looking for some advice about the best way to deal with it. Was worried the drainage would undermine his foundation or flood his basement. You know Norman Lutz? The developer?"

"No. Haven't heard of him."

"He developed the Estates some years back, and there have been a lot of problems up there related to how he laid out the roads and lots. Anyway, Jorgenson tried to get Lutz to fix the collapsed culvert under the road that would have pulled road drainage away from his property and down the hill at the end of Lakeview Terrace, but Lutz refused. Jorgenson tried to get the town's officials involved in resolving the issue, but once the town had signed off on the subdivision, they had little interest in mediating the dispute.

"I suggested he try a sump pump if he was concerned about water getting into the basement. Sold him a mid-range model and told him how to install it. Know anything about sump pumps?"

"Can't say that I do."

"You have to place them near an electric source, then dig a hole for the pump. If you hit ledge, you're out of luck. Told him he could bring the unit back, but he hasn't. Don't know how that worked out for him. The only alternative would be a retaining wall to prevent the drainage from impacting the foundation."

"Anything else?"

"He was a man of few words, but I thought he was a nice guy. When he saw the bird feeders I sell, he asked if I had any interest in selling birdhouses at the store. I told him to bring one in and we'd talk."

"You said you were trying to get more of them, so I guess the birdhouses were nice?"

"Beautiful. And unique. Sold quite a few of them. If you come across any finished ones while you're working on his estate, I'd love to buy them."

"I'll remember that. Anything else you can tell me?"

"Not that I can think of," he answered, taking another sip of his coffee.

"Thanks for all you've told me. I'll keep an eye out for the birdhouses. Have a great day."

"You too."

The sky was a deep blue with small puffs of clouds, the sun shining, belying the frigid temperature and periodic gusts of wind so typical of blustery March in New England. Even though she had worn her fleece-lined jacket, Gaby shivered as she hiked up the hill toward Town Hall, which sat on a knoll about eighteen yards from the grocery and hardware stores. She paused to pull the knit beanie down over her long black hair, covering her ears in an effort to stay warm during the short walk.

Woodson Falls Town Hall had been built in the '40s, when the town's population was below 800. Now the brown-sided building's few offices were bursting at the seams, with several employees sharing space originally designed for one.

Gaby's first stop, the town clerk's office, was located directly across from the building's entrance and served as an unofficial reception center for residents, visitors, contractors, real estate agents, attorneys and others with business to do in Town Hall. A massive black antique safe stood to the left of the counter that separated visitors from the main office space and the vault housing the town's records. The safe's heavy door was opened to display brochures about Woodson Falls and the state park, as well as area maps, fishing license applications, and other commonly requested information. Town Clerk Martha Rubin was at her desk, which overflowed with files and paperwork, her head in her hands.

"Martie," Gaby exclaimed. "What's going on?"

Martha had only recently taken over the office of town clerk, elected to the position after Mildred Pearson, the previous town clerk, resigned under the cloud of a pending investigation into her possible embezzlement of town funds. Her resignation had triggered the need for a special election, leaving coverage of the office to Mildred's assistant, Patty Truscott, in the interim.

"Oh! Hi, Gaby. Caught me in a down moment," Martha said, mustering a smile. "I just can't seem to get caught up on all these old filings." She waved an arm over the files threatening to cascade from each side of her desk. "I don't think much got done while Mildred was fending off questions about how she was managing the town's special funds. She held such tight control of the workflow that Patty never learned the nuts and bolts of the job. She feels bad that there's such a backlog, but she doesn't know where to start. I'm not sure I do either, though I took the classes to qualify for this office." She sighed then added, "I always wanted to serve in this position, offer a smiling face to the public, but now I wonder. I can't manage to get out from under this mess. Sorry. What can I do for you?"

"I'm fine, Martie. Just checking the land records," said Gaby as she headed for the vault. As a familiar face in Town Hall, she was granted access to areas like the vault without the need to show identification.

"Is this where we come for a marriage license?" asked a nervous young man who had trailed into the office behind Gaby, a pretty girl close to his side, their hands entwined.

Martha rose from her seat and approached the counter to help the young couple. "This is the place," she said with a smile.

# Chapter 4

ONCE IN THE VAULT, GABY ENTERED JORGENSON'S NAME INTO the computer system to pull up the deed for 16 Lakeview Terrace, which she would need for filing with the probate court. After clicking the button that sent the deed to the printer, she took the time to search for any information on possible liens against the property. She found a reference to a construction mortgage that had been released a year ago as well as the notice alerting anyone interested in the property about the pending legal action. There were no other liens, and the default judgment hadn't been filed on the land records yet. *Probably lost in that pile on Martie's desk, along with the death certificate.*

Curious, Gaby entered the name of Jorgenson's next-door neighbor into the system. Loomis and his wife had purchased their building lot six years ago, just four years before Jorgenson acquired his lot. It was unlikely Loomis would have prevailed in an adverse possession claim against his neighbor if he had appeared in court. Connecticut law required that the right to use all or a portion of another person's property, usually claimed in order to travel over the other property, would not be granted unless the claimant, in this case, Loomis, had used the property without interruption by the owner for a full fifteen years. Still, such a claim followed the land rather than its owners. There might be some legitimate basis for the action.

Grabbing the printout of the deed, Gaby paid the fifty cents for the copy and waved goodbye to Martie, who was now assisting an attorney in filing the paperwork to record a property transfer following its sale. Then she proceeded to the assessor's office around the corner to make note of the valuation of the Jorgenson property in the most recent revaluation on which property taxes were levied.

The office door was ajar but, despite the distinct odor of cigar smoke lingering in the air, Zeth Osborn, the assessor, was nowhere to be found. Gaby was just as glad not to have to deal with the often-surly man. Most townspeople couldn't wait until Osborn retired. Making a copy of the field card recording the dimensions of the building along with the valuation, Gaby plunked down fifty cents for the copy and quickly exited the office, heading to the friendlier territory of the tax collector, Sally Gorman.

"Sally! How are you doing? How are the kids?" Gaby stopped in the doorway and looked around. "Where is everyone?" she asked, surprised that Sally was alone in the office, which she shared with the building official, health director, land use enforcement officer, and fire marshal.

"Out doing their jobs for a change," Sally responded. "And I'm fine. So are Ryan and Ali. They miss you."

"I miss them too." Gaby occasionally stayed with Sally's children while Sally took classes at Prescott Community College with the goal of eventually earning a degree in accounting. Like Gaby, she was a young widow. Her husband had been killed while serving with the Marine Corps in Afghanistan.

"Come on over for dinner sometime soon. The kids would love to see you." Sally made her way toward the counter. "What can I do for you?"

"I'm checking up on whether Pieter Jorgenson was current on his taxes. Sixteen Lakeview Terrace."

"Was?"

"He died recently and Judge Taylor asked me to handle the estate."

"First I've heard of it."

"Died in New York, apparently with no relatives. Could you also check on any vehicles he might have had?"

Sally's fingers sailed across the computer keyboard. "Found it," she said. "Now I remember. Always paid his taxes with a money order, which I found odd. Yup, two vehicles, a Ford pickup and an old Jeep. No boat though. Current on taxes. Want a printout?"

"That would be great. Thanks so much," said Gaby, taking the information from Sally and opening the small change purse she carried, full of quarters, payment for the inevitable copies of documents needed for her work. Laying yet another fifty cents on the counter, she added, "Dinner Saturday evening okay? I'll bring my famous double chocolate brownies."

"Wonderful. About six? The kids'll be thrilled to see you."

"See you then," Gaby said with a wave as she exited the office.

Her business in Town Hall done for now, Gaby consulted her watch. *Whoa! My conversations with Frank and the folks at Mike's Place this morning really ate up a lot of time!* As she left the building, she weighed skipping lunch and driving up to Lakeview Terrace versus heading to Prescott to pick up the death certificate and eat at the Greene Bean, her favorite Prescott restaurant. Her growling stomach made the decision for her.

The Greene Bean was an unlikely success story for a restaurant in mostly blue-collar Prescott. Serving organic food from six in the morning until three in the afternoon, Judy Greene's storefront bistro had attracted a broad following, with Gaby one of the more loyal fans.

As she savored her rosemary-glazed ham and brie panini and side salad, Gaby considered the information she had gathered at Town Hall for the Jorgenson estate and what she still needed to learn. An estate like this, where she had never met the decedent, was like a scavenger hunt. A mental checklist of items she would need to cover would guide her as she tracked down and put together the pieces that had constituted Jorgenson's life before he died.

She would need to identify any assets other than the house and vehicles, which she would have to secure against theft or vandalism, neither of which was likely in quiet Woodson Falls. She would need to be on the lookout for possible "laughing cousins," distant relatives who might end up inheriting what Jorgenson owned if there was no will, while at the same time keeping an eye out for a will that would direct Jorgenson's assets to the people he had identified.

Sipping the last of her peppermint tea, Gaby picked up the check and opened her purse.

"Care to share?" A plate sporting an over-sized oatmeal chocolate chip cookie followed the deep voice. "It's still warm."

"Bill," she said, looking up at the tall, distinguished man who was offering the treat. "Have a seat. You've saved me a phone call."

"About the Jorgenson estate?"

"Yes! How did you know?" Gaby broke off a piece of the gooey cookie, popping it into her mouth. "Mmm... Delicious!"

"I asked Bud Taylor if he'd appoint someone to handle the estate so my client could make good on his judgment. The attorney who was handling the land dispute doesn't do probate work, and I mentioned your name to Bud."

"What's your client looking for?"

"Just an easement over a corner of Jorgenson's property. He was hoping the threat of a lawsuit would convince Jorgenson to settle, but the guy wanted his day in court. Claimed Loomis was causing water damage to his property. Eroding the foundation or some such."

Gaby had met Bill Harrison at several local bar meetings. He had a highly successful land use practice and was reputed to be a very eligible bachelor. He'd asked Gaby out on several occasions. She liked him enough, but was reluctant to resume dating and even more reluctant to date another lawyer. While she was careful not to allow her law practice to consume her life, she knew this wasn't the case for most career attorneys.

"How did you learn Jorgenson had died?"

"His attorney, Paul Evans, called me. The police notified him of his client's death when they found Evans' business card in Jorgenson's wallet. Paul told me he suspected the case was a loser, despite some potential claims in Jorgenson's favor. But Jorgenson had insisted on moving forward rather than settling the case. Without a client, Evans couldn't pursue the other claims, and we agreed that a default judgment requiring Jorgenson to grant an easement to Loomis at fair market value was a better result than withdrawing the case.

"All of the property owners along that side of Lakeview Terrace have granted easements to their neighbors given the botched job the surveyor did in laying out the lots along that stretch."

"What do you mean?" Gaby asked, breaking off another piece of cookie.

"Have you been up there yet?"

When Gaby shook her head, Harrison continued. "All of the properties on the lake-side of the road are below the grade of the road." He pulled out a pen and turned his napkin over. "Each lot was drawn parallel to the road," he said, drawing the configuration on the napkin. "The slope up to the road is too steep for a driveway given the size of the lots. The only way to access each property is across a corner of the adjacent property, in this case, toward the end of the road. The lots would never be approved under today's zoning regulations, but this subdivision pre-dates zoning, so no one considered the consequences of the layout, which I'm sure was done to maximize the number of lots along that stretch. Angling the properties would have solved the problem but cost the developer one or two lots. Instead, each of the property owners along that side of the road had to purchase an easement from his neighbor to access his own property. It worked fine for everyone except the owner of the first lot along that stretch, who needed to purchase an easement from his neighbor but had none to sell."

"So, what was the issue?" Gaby asked, licking a bit of chocolate from her finger, then wiping her hands on her napkin.

"Jorgenson's lot is the last on the road, so he didn't need an easement in order to exit his property and didn't want to give in to Loomis' demands," Bill explained.

Gaby groaned inwardly with the news that Jorgenson's property was the last one on the road. "Thanks for sharing your cookie and for the background information, Bill. I'll be in touch about the easement after I have a handle on the estate."

She knew better than to commit to executing the easement on behalf of the estate. She'd need to determine the value of the easement to negotiate a reasonable compensation to Jorgenson's estate for granting it, as well as explore any counter-claims that might be raised against Loomis since her fiduciary duty as estate administrator would be to act in the best interests of the estate.

Leaving the restaurant, Gaby walked the short distance to the probate court, where Jorgenson's death certificate was waiting for her. Tucking it into her briefcase, she headed back to her car and to Woodson Falls. She'd stop at home to let Kat out and then check out the Jorgenson property.

## Chapter 5

GABY TOOK ROUTE 41 BACK TO WOODSON FALLS, HEADING toward her cottage on Beaver Trail. As she drove along winding Pine Hill Road, she found herself behind a rural mail truck as it made frequent stops, the curves in the road making it unsafe to pass.

*Poor timing,* she thought, reminded to check Jorgenson's mailbox when she finally got to the house. Accumulated mail was likely to contain bills and other correspondence that would help in piecing together the details of Jorgenson's life before his sudden death.

Arriving home, Gaby opened the front door, clinging to the doorframe as Kat came bounding toward her in an exuberant greeting. She pulled a biscuit from the small bag of treats she had picked up at Mike's Place, rewarding Kat for waiting so patiently for her return, then giving the dog a hug and a pat on the head. Gobbling down the treat, Kat dashed toward the woods to do her business. Gaby was checking for phone messages when Kat wandered back into the house, rolling over to invite a tummy rub that Gaby was happy to deliver.

"Want to come along?" Ready to finally explore the Lakeview Terrace house, Gaby gestured toward the open car door, inviting Kat to jump in, then followed the dog into the car and backed out of her driveway, retracing her way to Route 41.

Woodson Lake sparkled in the distance as Gaby drove north and past the state park on her way to Woodson Lake Estates. The town's one traffic light turned green as she approached the intersection where Sawmill, Pleasantview and Farm Roads forked off Route 41. She turned right, heading up Pleasantview toward the Estates. Kat hung her head out the open window, while Gaby cranked up the heat, shivering in the frigid air.

Gaby had wondered how she would get past the gate to Woodson Lake Estates. Fortunately, a delivery truck was driving out just as she approached the gate, allowing her to pass through before the gates closed again. She made a mental note to ask someone for the gate code since it was likely she would be coming up to Lakeview Terrace several times in the next few months.

Having reviewed her map before setting out, Gaby had only a vague idea of where she would find Lakeview Terrace in the subdivision's warren of dirt roads. The few weathered signs that stood at some of the intersections were of little help in guiding her to her destination, serving only to confuse her as she rumbled along the deeply rutted roads.

Once she turned into Lakeview Terrace, Gaby parked at number twelve and got out of the car to hike the rest of the way down to Jorgenson's house, leaving Kat behind in the car. She had no intention of getting trapped trying to turn at the end of the road. Most of the houses she passed looked closed up for the winter, their owners likely having fled south for the worst of the winter months or holed up in New York City apartments, where snow removal was managed by someone else. They'd straggle back to Woodson Falls once the weather turned nice again.

She made her way down the steep road, which narrowed to nearly nothing before ending at a cliff. Happy that she had decided to leave the car farther up the road, she turned to look at the rather nondescript house before going down the driveway. The few windows stared like unseeing eyes, shades drawn, shutters a mildewed white against the pea-green aluminum siding topped by an asphalt shingle roof, gutters filled with leaves.

As she proceeded down the steep driveway, she had a better appreciation of what Bill had told her about the difficulties in accessing these lots given the grade of the hill on which the houses had to be built.

The driveway ended as a breezeway, a garage on the right, the house on the left. The remnants of the disputed cement wall Judge Taylor had mentioned were visible on the far side of the garage, with a paved driveway running through and connecting into Jorgenson's. It looked like Loomis hadn't waited for an easement to be negotiated.

Gaby peeked into the garage, spotting an Army-issue jeep through the grimy windows as well as mountains of presumably empty gallon-sized plastic water bottles. She wondered if the house had a functioning well and septic and, if so, whether the water was potable. Why else would Jorgenson be using so many jugs of bottled water?

Looking over the side of the breezeway to the steep hillside below, Gaby saw that the level below this one had walls of poured cement. A deck surrounded this lower level of the house. A third level, most likely the basement, ran below the deck and appeared to lead to a small cleared area in the midst of the tall trees that marched down the hillside to the lake below. There was no clear path to the lake, the hill steep enough to challenge even a mountain goat.

Turning to the door to the house, Gaby tried the doorknob. Despite the resident state trooper's frequent notices in the local paper warning homeowners to secure their houses when they were out, many in Woodson Falls left their front doors unlocked when they were away. Not Jorgenson. The house was tightly locked.

Gaby poked around a bit, looking for a likely hiding place for the house key, recalling her law school professor's question the first day of the estate administration and taxation course she had elected to take.

"You've been assigned by the court to administer an estate. What's the first thing you do as the personal representative of the estate with a duty to the beneficiaries?"

Her classmates had voiced various responses, none of which hit the mark.

"The first thing you do," Professor Whitlock had said, "is to secure the house to protect it against theft or vandalism. So, you've got to find the key."

Gaby tried the door to the garage, thinking the house key might be hanging on a hook inside, but it, too, was locked. She turned when she heard someone calling down to her from the road.

"What are you doing down there, Miss? That man will have a conniption fit if he finds you here. Doesn't take kindly to people on his property."

"Hi there!" Gaby called, heading partway back up the driveway to see a middle-aged woman wearing a brown wool coat with a faux fur collar standing at the side of the road looking down at her. She held a tan bundle of fur in her arms that turned its black eyes toward Gaby as she continued toward the woman.

"How adorable! A Yorkshire terrier, right?" she asked as she neared the woman, putting out her hand to allow the small dog to sniff.

"Yes, this is my Fifi. She's a good dog, aren't you, lovey?" the woman said, nuzzling the dog's head.

"I'm Gabriella Quinn, a local attorney," Gaby said. "I was asked by the probate court to handle Mr. Jorgenson's estate. He died while he was in New York."

"Oh, my! Hadn't heard that."

"I was wondering if you knew whether Mr. Jorgenson left a key with a neighbor. I'll need to get into the house. By the way, what's your name?"

"Not that I'm aware of." Putting the dog down, she crossed her arms and looked at Gaby. "Not to speak ill of the dead," she said, "but he was *not* a nice person."

"What do you mean, Mrs...?"

"Markham. Angela Markham. Well, a while back, last summer I think, I was walking my little dog here. My friend, Frieda, was with me. She was visiting from Dayton, Ohio. We go way, way back. We were in high school together. Remained friends ever since. Try to get together at least once a year."

"You were walking your dog... and?"

"Yes, and Fifi stepped into Jorgenson's driveway, sniffing like dogs do, then, uh... well... did what dogs do right then and there. As I picked it up... I always carry a plastic baggie, you know. I'm a good citizen that way. Well, that man comes storming up the driveway, chasing us and shouting that he'd kill my Fifi if he ever saw her on his property again. He was always yelling at folks and threatening to sue them. Frieda saw what happened. We were both scared to death. Who can't love a little dog like my Fifi?"

"She *is* adorable. Did anything else happen?"

"He sent me a letter. Threatened to take legal action if I ever let Fifi come near his property again. I sent him a note back. Pleasant enough, although I told him Fifi thought he should take some spelling lessons."

"Do you still have his letter?"

"No. I let Fifi poop on it. Like I said, he is... was... not a nice man. You won't find many folks here who liked him... or knew anything about the man," she said, turning to head toward her house across the street with Fifi trotting behind her. "Good luck to you."

"Thanks for talking with me, Mrs. Markham. You have a nice day," Gaby called. Turning back toward the house, she checked the mailbox to the left of the driveway. All that was in it was one of the post office's yellow cards indicating there was too much mail to fit in the box. She'd have to visit with the postmaster to retrieve the mail once she was formally appointed by the probate court as the administrator of Jorgenson's estate.

Gaby hiked back to her car. *Guess I'll have to call Rusty Dolan to break into the house.*

# Chapter 6

"HI, RUSTY. GABY QUINN. HOW ARE YOU?"

"Hey, Gaby! It's been a while. Doin' okay. How's with you?"

"I'm fine. And Maggie?"

"She's been enjoying the winter weather, but she's ready for the flowers to bloom, if not for the summer heat. What can I do for you?"

John Patrick "Rusty" Dolan, Jr., a fixture in Woodson Falls, has lived there all his life except for the four years he served with the Marines in Iraq. When he came home, he married his childhood sweetheart, Maggie McGoldrick. They live in the same small farmhouse his forebears had built centuries ago, before the country was born. When Maggie had a skiing accident that fractured her pelvis and left her in a wheelchair, Rusty put his heart and soul into remodeling the place so they could remain there together.

Well-muscled and six-foot-two, the red hair that gave him his nickname now spattered with grey, Rusty is a man nobody fools with, a beloved tough guy with a heart of gold. Like his father and grandfather before him, Rusty works as a carpenter and handyman—one of those people who seemingly can do anything. It's a job he enjoys and that pays the bills while giving him the flexibility to care for Maggie.

"I'm involved with the estate of a man who lived up in Woodson Lake Estates. I can't find a key to the house and was hoping you'd be able to get into the place, then change the locks to secure the house."

"Sure. Glad to help. Can I meet you up there later this morning? Say, ten o'clock?"

"That would be great. It's Lakeview Terrace. Last house on the right. Number sixteen. Do you happen to have the gate code? I'll need it when I go back up there."

"Yeah. It's 0216. See you there."

Gaby had skipped dinner the evening before, snacking on a protein bar, so after her morning run with Kat, she fed the dog, filled her water bowl, and headed to Peggy's Sunshine Café for breakfast.

Peggy's offered a wide-open space, booths along the walls, two- and four-seat tables scattered in the center, a long counter to the right of the front door. Gaby slipped into a booth and glanced at the menu even though she knew she'd have the same breakfast she always had at Peggy's. Long-time waitress Helen wandered over, coffee pot in hand, filling Gaby's cup without asking.

"Same breakfast, hon? Two scrambled, bacon, biscuits, no potatoes?"

Gaby chuckled. "Too predictable, I guess. Someday I'll surprise you, Helen, and order a stack of pancakes, though Peggy's biscuits are hard to resist."

"Bacon on the side?"

"You know me too well. Not the healthiest choice, but I can't resist Peggy's bacon any more than her biscuits."

She flipped through the local paper left by a previous diner, glancing nervously every now and then at a tall man sitting at the counter who looked vaguely familiar, wondering where she might have seen him before. She quickly ducked her head when the stranger looked over at her, allowing her long hair to cover her scarred cheek as she turned back to the newspaper.

When Helen brought her breakfast, she asked, "That guy eating at the counter. Do you know him?"

"Not really. He started coming in a few weeks ago. Bought the old Haverson Place at the north end of town. Fixing it up. Not married. Didn't like me asking him questions, it seemed, so I don't know much else—not even his name. Not one for chatting, and the look he gave me when I asked him where he was from... Well, it was scary.

"Enjoy," Helen said, setting Gaby's plate down. "Let me know when you need a refill on that coffee."

"Thanks, Helen."

As she ate breakfast, Gaby mentally catalogued the things she'd be looking for at Jorgenson's house, trying to ignore her racing heart. She held up her hand when Helen came by with the coffee pot and the check.

"Thanks, Helen, but I'm full. A third cup of coffee would give me the jitters," she said with a smile.

Leaving the restaurant, Gaby noticed a white van with dull orange New York license plates parked right outside and wondered if the van belonged to the stranger at the counter. She couldn't shake the feeling that she'd seen him before, her anxiety mounting and urging her to run away.

*Couldn't be the guy who killed Joe in New York. Couldn't be.* Gaby had never been sure why the knife-wielding stranger had attacked her and Joe, whether it had been a random assault or a targeted attack against one of them for some unknown reason. Shaking her head to clear her mind before it drifted back to those dark days, she ducked into her Subaru and drove up to Lakeview Terrace to meet Rusty.

She parked a few houses up the road from Jorgenson's and walked toward number sixteen, spotting Rusty's truck near the driveway. He wasn't in the truck. She made her way down the driveway and looked over the fence at the back of the breezeway between the garage and the house. As she stood there in the morning sun, wondering where he might be, Rusty opened the front door.

"Hi, Gaby. Got here a little early so I thought I'd look around. Interesting place. Guy must have been salvaging odds and ends from old houses and offices. The second floor is filled with all kinds of stuff.

"Craziest thing. The guy's got a deadbolt lock up here, which I couldn't get past, but there's a flimsy lock on the basement door. Easy to open. Just used a credit card. Probably figured no one could access the house that way."

"The basement door? The house is surrounded by woods, and the hill to the lake is awfully steep. How'd you get down there?"

"Marine secret. I'm going to head down to the hardware store and pick up a few locksets for the doors. Why don't you look around while I'm gone?"

"Before you leave, would you mind giving me a sense of the layout of the house, so I know what I'm walking into?"

"Sure. The house is built into the side of the hill—a pretty steep one at that. It's designed like an upside-down house, with the living area on the top floor. Usually, the lower floor contains bedrooms, but in this house, the level below this one is a large room, sort of like a big man cave."

"And the basement? You mentioned the door. Is it a full basement? Livable?"

"Probably half of the area is hillside. The floor is dirt, so no, it would take additional work to make it livable. The mechanicals— the heating system and water heater—have been mounted on cement slabs. There are some shovels and rakes down there, and the floor's been disturbed where it looks like the owner tried to dig a hole to accommodate a sump pump. Must have abandoned the idea of a pump to handle drainage. Maybe hit ledge. There's a boxed unit down there, but it hasn't been opened."

"Thanks, Rusty."

"See you in a bit," Rusty called, waving as he headed up the driveway.

Pushing the front door wider, Gaby scanned an open room that stretched to the end of the house before stepping inside, gently closing the door behind her. Her attention was drawn to the span of picture windows along the lake-side of the room, providing a spectacular view of Woodson Lake as well as the waterfall. Her eyes were drawn upward to the long shelf above the windows, which held a row of homemade birdhouses of various shapes and sizes, all roofed with the same asphalt shingles as the house. Centered just below the window-sills were a sizable picnic table and bench neatly arrayed with wood-working tools and materials as well as what looked like a partially finished birdhouse. She noticed several small, carved figures lying toward the back of the table and leaned to reach for them.

One figure was a seven-inch-tall man dressed in a short-sleeved blue chambray shirt and white twill overalls. An oddly-shaped metal rod, close to three inches in length, was stuck into the top of the over-alls. She pulled it out and turned it over in her hand, wondering what it might represent. The figure's features were carefully carved and the limbs fully jointed. Some sort of paint or stain had been used to indicate hair and lips, the figure's boots stained the same dark brown color as the hair. The clothing had been hand-stitched, with the over-all straps glued in place. *A self-portrait?* Gaby wondered, as she laid down the figure and picked up one of the other dolls.

This figure, clearly a boy, was about four inches high and dressed in a plaid shirt and denim pants. It had the same carefully carved features and fully jointed limbs as the man, but with yellow paint for hair. Four other figures, two girls and two more boys, varied in height and dress but were as carefully made as the first two figures she had looked at. Intrigued, Gaby set them aside on the table and turned to look at the rest of the room.

Along the wall where she had entered was a rudimentary kitchen, some battered cookware on the range, unopened gallon-sized water bottles arranged along the counter, cabinets above. A transistor radio stood at the end of the counter nearest the windows.

Two doorways interrupted the wall opposite the windows. Centered between the doorways was a tall oak filing cabinet—a likely place to locate the papers Gaby was looking for. She needed to identify the assets of the estate as well as any unpaid bills. There might even be a copy of Jorgenson's will filed in there. But before she delved into the contents of the filing cabinet, Gaby wanted to complete her survey of this floor of the house.

A chair and side table stood close to the front door. At the end of the room were a sofa upholstered in a drab brown, two end tables holding reading lamps, a coffee table, and side chairs arranged on a braided rag rug. The sofa and chairs were piled high with empty gallon-sized plastic water bottles. One of the end tables held a telephone, hard-wired into the oak-paneled wall, as well as a stack of magazines. The other held a mug, half-filled with coffee, a film coating the top of the liquid. Stacks of magazines occupied space on the coffee table and were piled on the floor beneath the table.

Gaby ventured into the hallway, feeling a bit unsettled by her intrusion on the dead stranger's property. There, she discovered two bedrooms, a bathroom and a door that presumably led to the lower levels of the house. The bedroom to the right contained a narrow single bed that had been neatly made with a wool blanket and a pillow. A tall steel locker stood to the right of the bed, a straight-back cane chair to the left. A bureau with six drawers was the only other furnishing in this spartan room. No pictures adorned the walls and the top of the bureau was bare except for a hand-wound alarm clock that had stopped at 6:19.

The second bedroom was dominated by a double bed with a carved wooden headboard and covered with a quilt. A stuffed teddy bear sat between the bed's two pillows. A framed picture of a lake scene hung above the bed. Two large packing boxes stood in front of a dresser, the top of which held a framed photograph of a young blonde woman and a small, dark-haired boy of about seven, a basket filled with sewing items, and a hairbrush and comb. Gaby peeked into one of the cardboard boxes, which appeared to contain magazine and newspaper clippings.

A few dresses hung in the narrow closet; women's shoes were lined up on the closet shelf. Gaby wondered just who had occupied this room. *Probably his mother,* she thought, remembering her conversation with Frank Pastore, *but who knows.* Based on her brief conversation with the neighbor, Angela Markham, and others in town, it seemed no one knew much about Jorgenson's personal life.

Returning to the hallway, Gaby briefly explored the small bathroom that stood at one end of the hallway. The bathroom held a toilet, sink and a bathtub that was filled with the ubiquitous plastic bottles. Gaby turned on a faucet, but no water flowed. The medicine cabinet above the sink held shaving cream, a safety razor, toothpaste and toothbrush, as well as a bottle of aspirin and another of antacid tablets. Two towels and a washcloth hung on a rail screwed into the wall.

At the other end of the hallway was a door. Gaby opened it, eyed the wooden staircase and the darkness below, and decided to wait until another day to explore the lower levels of the house.

# Chapter 7

RUSTY CAME BACK FROM TOWN, STARTLING GABY AS SHE returned to the main room to retrieve the briefcase she had brought with her.

"Finding what you need?" he asked before heading down to the basement level.

"Just getting started," she replied. "I'm surprised things are so neatly organized inside. Except, of course, for all those empty water bottles. I'm just hoping it will be fairly easy to locate the information I'm looking for."

"Good luck with that. I'll just change the lock downstairs then come back up to do the front door and garage. See you in a bit."

She had brought her oversized briefcase with her, intending to load it with any useful documents she found in the house so she could review them in the comfort of her own office. She carried it to the first bedroom she had entered, flipping the light switch that turned on an overhead light. The electricity was still on.

Beginning with the dresser, Gaby pulled out each drawer. The top drawer held a toiletry kit as well as a small box of photos and an address book, both of which Gaby slipped into her briefcase. The other drawers contained clothing that was neatly folded and sorted into like piles: underwear, socks, handkerchiefs in one drawer; T-shirts and short-sleeved shirts in the next; long-sleeved shirts and sweaters in the next two; a set of sheets and a blanket in the lowest drawer. She flipped through each pile to see if something might be hidden within the clothing or at the bottom of one of the piles, but came up empty except for random scraps of cloth between each of the shirts and sweaters that looked like remnants cut from larger pieces of various fabrics. Gaby shook her head, puzzled by the odd discovery.

She turned next to the steel locker. Trousers and overalls hung on hooks, pockets containing only loose change. *Wallet's probably been secured by the police along with Jorgenson's other personal effects*, Gaby thought, although she was aware that items often had a way of disappearing when someone—dead or alive—was transported by ambulance to a city hospital, which she assumed was what happened with Jorgenson.

A pair of work boots stood on the floor of the locker, heavy woolen socks stuffed into them. A shelf at the top of the locker held a small, ring-bound notebook and pencil as well as several pages clipped together that appeared to have been torn from the yellow pages of a telephone book. Gaby slipped the notebook and yellow pages into her briefcase. As she shut the locker door, she noticed a calendar hanging inside. There were penciled notations on the top page, so she added the calendar to her briefcase.

There was nothing else of interest in the room. She turned off the light and moved on to the other bedroom. Sufficient sunlight filtered through the drawn shade to examine the contents of this room without turning on a light. Beyond the dresses and shoes she had seen earlier, there was nothing in the closet. The dresser drawers that weren't blocked by the cardboard boxes contained women's underwear and other clothing, along with evidence that a mouse had lounged there at some point in time, nestled in a pile of panties. The boxes were too heavy to push out of the way, so she deferred looking into the remaining drawers until another day.

As Gaby moved on to the oak filing cabinet in the main living area, she could see her breath in the still air and wondered if Jorgenson had run out of heating oil or simply winterized the house and drained the pipes, which would explain the dry faucet. *Either that or the property still lacks a well.*

The files in the cabinet were neatly labeled and organized, so it was relatively easy for Gaby to pick and choose what she would take for further examination when she returned home. Rusty came back upstairs as she was working her way through the second drawer.

"How's it going?" he asked.

"Slowly, but I seem to be finding the basics I need. How's it going with the locks?"

"Almost done."

"Before you go, would you mind shifting some boxes in one of the bedrooms so I can go through the dresser drawers next time I'm here?" Gaby showed Rusty what she meant.

"Sure thing," Rusty replied, easily moving the boxes away from the dresser. "Anything else?"

"Not right now. Thanks."

Gaby went back into the main room and continued with her search, her briefcase bulging with the many files she thought might be helpful in processing the estate. Rusty was changing the lock on the front door when Gaby finished with the filing cabinet. Scanning the big room, she couldn't see anywhere else to search, so she returned to the table in front of the windows, looking again at the carved figures.

"Here's a set of keys that will open all three locks," Rusty said, dropping a ring of keys into her hand. "They're all the same. Any one of them will open any of the locks. I'll keep a set just in case you want me to get back into the house without you."

"Can I pay you for your time and the locksets now, or do you want to bill me?" she responded.

"I'll send you the bill. Let me know if there's anything else you'll be needing."

"Any idea what this might represent?" she asked, picking up the figure of the man and pulling out the metal rod that had been placed in the figure's overalls.

Rusty took the rod in his hand, turning it over. "Looks like an old spud bar. It would be used to pry shingles off a roof. Neat little thing. Wonder how he made it?" he said, handing the tool back to Gaby. "Maybe the guy was a roofer. Haven't seen this type of spud bar since I tagged along with my grandfather on odd jobs."

"Thanks. I'll let you know if I can confirm your guess. And thanks for coming this morning. I really wanted to get started on this case before something else came up."

"Take care now," Rusty called in parting.

"Give Maggie my best, and thanks again," Gaby replied.

She added the figure and its curious bar to her briefcase. Before leaving the house, she looked around, thinking about what she hadn't come across. No television, no wireless router indicating a computer somewhere in the house, no cell phone charger, although Jorgenson might charge a cell phone in his car—or another house or apartment, for that matter. She hadn't been surprised to see the landline since cell service was spotty at best all through Woodson Falls. Even this high up, her own cell phone indicated no service was available.

As she made her way to the front door, Gaby glanced down at the newspaper on the side table near the door. It was opened to a story about the search for a child who had been abducted. The paper was dated January 15th, a few weeks before Jorgenson had died. *How sad.* She knew many such abductions ended badly and said a small prayer that the child had been found. Locking the door behind her, she headed up the steep driveway and on to her car.

*Next stop, the post office.*

Last night, Gaby had completed the application to be formally appointed administrator of Jorgenson's estate by the probate court using the information from the death certificate as well as the bits and pieces she had gleaned from her visit to Town Hall. She planned to mail the application to the court from the post office, which would give her the opportunity to inquire about Jorgenson's mail. If she was lucky enough to talk with the right postal worker, she might even be able to get the mail before having formal authorization from the court—one of the benefits of practicing law in a small town, where personal relationships often trumped formalities.

Arriving at the post office on her way home from the Estates, Gaby saw that Mrs. Browning's daughter-in-law Karen was manning the counter.

"Hi, Karen. How's everything?"

"Just fine, Gaby. How can I help you?"

"Well, first, is there enough postage on this?" Gaby asked, handing over the manila envelope containing the application to the probate court for the estate, along with supporting material she had gathered at Town Hall.

"Just right. New case?"

"Yes, an estate. Pieter Jorgenson at 16 Lakeview Terrace. I picked this up from his mailbox," Gaby responded, handing over the yellow card. "I'm wondering if I could access his accumulated mail."

"Evie wondered what was going on. He didn't often let his mail accumulate. How'd he die? He was still young, no?"

"Yes, quite young. Not sure exactly what happened, but he died last month in New York City."

"Let me see what I can find in back."

After a few minutes, Karen returned carrying a pile of mail secured by a large rubber band. "This is it," she said, handing the pile over to Gaby. "I'll direct any additional mail to your address. Just bring in a copy of the probate authorization when you get it so we have it on file for when we're audited."

"Will do, and thanks a million. This will be a big help in sorting out the estate."

Relieved that she was able to get the mail without a hassle, Gaby stopped at Mike's Place to pick up a container of vegetable beef soup, just what she needed after working in Jorgenson's unheated house for several hours. She was looking forward to a warm shower and a hot bowl of soup before plunging into all the material she had collected.

# Chapter 8

THE SHRILL RING OF THE PHONE GREETED GABY AS SHE OPENED her front door. Kat gave her a welcoming bark, then ran outside. Placing the container of soup on the kitchen counter and dropping her briefcase and purse to the floor, she reached for the phone.

"Hello. Law offices, Gabriella…"

"Oh, Gaby! I'm so glad I finally got you. I've been calling all afternoon."

"Fran? What's going on?"

Gaby first met Fran Murphy at church, during the coffee hour following Sunday services. The two had joined forces occasionally to volunteer at various church functions.

"It's my son Walter. He's been arrested."

"My goodness!"

"I don't know what to do or who to call. I thought of you right away."

"I'll do what I can to help. What happened?"

"I just don't know. A state trooper came here looking for him, but Walter had left for the day. I thought he was going to work, but now I'm not sure where he might have been headed. The trooper wouldn't tell me what it's about, but I'm scared for Walter. He's my youngest. I don't think I told you that he has some mental health issues."

"No, I don't think so."

"Walter's fine when he takes his medication, but the pills make him feel sluggish, so he stops taking them every now and then. When he's off the medication, he feels invincible, and I have to admit he sometimes does stupid things. I don't know what happened, and I'm so worried. What should I do? You're the only lawyer I know. Can you help?"

"You think he's actually been arrested?"

"Yes. He called me from the police station in Prescott. His one phone call, I guess."

"I'll head to Prescott now. I'm not a criminal lawyer, but I'll do what I can and then try to scout out a good criminal attorney for you if that's needed."

"Please hurry."

"I'll give you a call when I sort this out."

Filling Kat's dinner dish and water bowl and putting the soup in the refrigerator, Gaby grabbed her purse and headed back out the door as Kat wandered in.

"I'll be home as fast as I can, Kat," she said, giving the dog a quick hug and a pat on the head.

Back in her car and headed to Prescott, Gaby wondered how she should approach the situation. Without knowing why Walter had been arrested, there was nothing on which to base even a rudimentary plan. Hopefully, she could keep Walter from spending the night in jail while she found a criminal attorney to take his case.

Gaby pulled into a parking space marked "Visitors" at the rear of the modern brick building that housed the Prescott police department. As she approached the glass-enclosed front desk, she wished she had thought to bring her briefcase as well as change into something a bit more formal than her slacks and pullover sweater. *Might have helped me look more like an attorney and less like a frantic sister or girlfriend.*

The grey-haired, overweight officer manning the desk looked up as Gaby approached the window. "Can I help you?"

"I'm an attorney, here to represent Walter Murphy. I understand he's being held here."

"Identification, please?"

Feeling totally out of her element, Gaby slipped her driver's license and attorney photo identification through the slot at the bottom of the window.

Picking them up slowly, the officer looked them over, glanced up at Gaby, then left his seat to saunter over to a computer, taking her documents with him and leaving Gaby waiting at the window. Several minutes passed before he returned.

"Wear this in a visible place while you're in the building," he said, passing a tag with her name and the number of her attorney license printed on it through the slot along with her identification. "Over there," he said, tilting his head to indicate a door to the right of the window. A buzzer sounded, allowing Gaby to enter the office. Once inside, she was fumbling to return her license and bar card to her wallet when a state trooper approached her.

"Here to see Murphy?"

Looking up, Gaby gazed into the trooper's piercing blue eyes. "Yes," she murmured. "Yes, please."

"New at this, huh?" he answered with a smile. "Right this way, Ms…?"

"Gabriella Quinn," she responded before the trooper had the chance to read her name on the badge. "Can you tell me what he's charged with?"

"Violating a restraining order. He was seen lurking in the parking lot at Walmart before the store opened this morning."

Gaby followed the trooper down a corridor lined with closed doors. "A restraining order?"

Stopping short and turning toward her, the trooper said, "I thought you were his lawyer."

"I'm a lawyer, but I don't handle criminal cases. Just helping his mother until she can find a criminal attorney."

"Oh. Well, my understanding is that Murphy used to work at Walmart as a stock clerk until he was fired for threatening other employees with a box cutter. He kept coming into the store, frightening employees as well as shoppers. Walmart petitioned for the restraining order. Murphy never showed up in court, so the court issued the order. He was served notice. He knew he wasn't supposed to be anywhere near the store. I know he has a psychiatric history, but that isn't an excuse for violating the order."

He opened one of the doors. "You can wait in here. I'll bring your client to you."

"Excuse me," Gaby said, looking up from the trooper's badge. "Officer Thomas? I saw Walter this morning when I was having breakfast at the Sunshine Café in Woodson Falls. Walter busses tables there. I left a little past nine-thirty. I don't see how he could have been in the Walmart parking lot. The Café opens at six."

"You sure about that?"

"Absolutely, but you might want to check with the Café's owner, Peggy Huntington, to verify that. Can I see Walter now?"

"I'll bring him to you."

Walter looked a bit disheveled and sleepy but otherwise unscathed by his most recent brush with the law.

"Hi, Walter. I'm Gaby Quinn. I'm an attorney in Woodson Falls. I know your mom from church, and she called me when she learned you had been arrested. Can you tell me what happened?"

"Didn't I see you this morning? At the Sunshine Café?"

"Yes. I was having breakfast. I saw you working there. Did you come in at your usual time?"

"Uh-huh. I come in at five-thirty to help set up then work until just before noon. I get a half-hour breakfast, which I usually eat out in the kitchen, like this morning."

"When did you leave work today?"

"I guess it was around quarter to twelve."

"And then? Where did you go from there?"

"Did my mother tell you about my problem?"

"Yes, she mentioned you have a psychiatric illness that requires medication."

"I haven't been feeling too good on the pills they gave me, so I came to the clinic here in Prescott after work to see if there was something wrong or if I could get a different medication."

"How did you know the police were looking for you? I know you didn't talk to your mother. She was frantic, not knowing where you were."

"The cops had called the clinic looking for me, and the nurse there let me know they had been asking if I'd been there, though she didn't know why. She said it would be best if I came to the police station to clear things up, but as soon as I got here, they arrested me, took my picture—I guess that's a mug shot?—and put me in a cell. I didn't know who to call, so I called Mom and I guess she called you. What happens now?"

"I told Officer Thomas that I saw you this morning at the Café. I'm guessing they'll check that out and then let us know what's next. You didn't go to Walmart this morning, did you, say before work?"

"Of course not! I know I'm not supposed to go there. And anyway, it wouldn't be open that early in the morning."

"How about after work?"

"I went straight to the clinic, and then here. Never even got lunch."

"I'm with you there," Gaby answered, her stomach growling.

It was late afternoon before a different officer came to the room where they were waiting and sat down with Gaby and Walter.

"Well, young man, it seems your alibi checked out. Your employer vouched for your presence this morning. Turns out that the person lurking in the Walmart parking lot looks a lot like you and this was a case of mistaken identity."

"That's a relief," sighed Walter.

"Are we free to go?" Gaby asked.

"You are, miss. We need to do the paperwork to process Murphy out of the system, which may take a while. Do you have a means of transportation home, young man?"

"Yes, sir. My car's outside," Walter responded.

Gaby turned to Walter. "I'll call your mother to let her know you'll be home soon," she said.

"Thanks for coming. And for all you've done for me."

"I'm just glad it turned out alright for you, Walter."

Back in the parking lot, Gaby called Fran to convey the good news that Walter was free to go and the charges against him were being dropped.

# Chapter 9

IT WAS DUSK WHEN GABY PULLED OUT OF THE POLICE STATION parking lot, that in-between time of day when it's difficult to distinguish shapes from shadows. Storm clouds had gathered while she was at the police station, darkening the sky more than usual. It had turned colder as the sun set; the drizzle shining against the pavement as the streetlights glowed along the road.

Back on Route 41 headed toward Woodson Falls, Gaby couldn't wait to get home, have a bite to eat, and settle in for a long sleep under her down comforter. She felt dead on her feet, relieved that she was able to keep Walter out of jail, but tired, cold and hungry.

Her wipers were set on intermittent to clear the drizzle that blurred her view of the two-lane, winding road, the swish of the blades threatening to lull her to sleep. She turned on the radio and cracked the driver's side window to get a flow of fresh air, hoping both would keep her from nodding off.

She felt the jarring thump against her door and heard the screech of metal on metal as her car lurched to the right and into the post-and-cable guardrail that ran along a steep embankment. Turning off the ignition as she turned on her emergency blinkers, Gaby caught a glimpse of a large light-colored vehicle racing up the road and disappearing into the night.

"Damn," she muttered under her breath.

Gaby opened the driver's-side door gingerly, afraid that any movement might send the car careening down the embankment. She heard a rasping creak as the door opened a few inches, then refused to move any further. Gaby slid out and onto the pavement, then reached in to grab her purse. The car was tilted to the right, held in place—at least for the time being—by the cable that prevented it from sliding down the embankment.

Taking out her cell phone, Gaby was dismayed to see the "No Signal" message. It was too far to walk home. She could only hope some traveler would see her blinkers and stop to help. She shivered in the cold, damp air, stamping her feet periodically to warm them. *Never mind the soup. I need a long hot soak in my bathtub.*

A half-hour or more passed before Gaby glimpsed lights heading toward her. She waved her arms, hoping the car would slow down.

"Can I help you?" called a male voice from within what looked like a police cruiser.

"Please! I was sideswiped and pushed into the guardrail. I'm afraid to try to drive."

The male voice got out of the car and approached Gaby.

"Officer Thomas! Where did you come from?"

"That you, Ms. Quinn? Are you hurt?"

"Not hurt. Jostled a bit and angry that someone would hit my car and just drive off into the dark without stopping to see what they hit. Thank goodness you happened along. But I thought you worked in Prescott. What are you doing out here?"

"Saving stranded drivers, looks like." He went over to Gaby's car, checked its angle, and said, "Good thing you didn't try to drive. Your vehicle is teetering on that embankment. I'll call for a tow and give you a lift home... or to wherever you were headed."

"Thank you, thank you, thank you. I'm cold, I'm hungry, and I'm beyond tired. A lift home would be great, Officer Thomas, if you have the time."

"Let's wait inside the cruiser until the tow truck gets here. This rain is starting to freeze, and you're shivering."

Inside the police cruiser, its headlights illuminated the meteor shower of freezing rain as it struck the windshield, the wipers keeping a steady beat that barely kept up with the rain, Gaby turned to the trooper. "What were you doing out here?"

"I took an extra shift to cover for the trooper assigned to patrol Woodson Falls this evening. His wife went into the hospital to deliver their first kid. Seemed like the right thing to do."

"I'm sure glad you were headed this way. Not much traffic on 41 this time of night. I'd have had to risk getting back into my car or freeze to death."

"Any idea what hit you?"

"I just had a glimpse of a large car or van—no headlights. I thought I caught sight of a New York plate, but no details. I haven't a clue why the driver didn't stop."

"We might be able to track it down, based on the damage done to your car, but it's a long shot."

"I figured as much. Thank goodness for insurance."

They were silent for a spell, then Gaby said, "Excuse me for asking, but you were in Prescott when I got to the police station. I didn't know the Prescott police department patrolled other towns. And I know they don't have state troopers as part of their force."

"They don't—on both counts. I'm the resident trooper for Woodson Falls. Prescott police didn't know where Murphy was and, since he lives in Woodson Falls, they asked me to track him down and bring him in. I was notified when he turned himself in at the station and came down to handle the paperwork. There's a lot of overlap like that."

"You're the new resident trooper for Woodson Falls? I knew Steve Dynow was leaving, but not who would take his place."

"Yeah. When Dynow retired, I put in for the position and was fortunate to get it, after my appointment met with the approval of Mayor Dunleavy. I just began here a few weeks ago."

"Then why were you on patrol this evening? I mean besides covering for someone else? Doesn't a resident trooper work mostly days?"

"When a trooper is assigned to a town—most often a small town like Woodson Falls that can't support its own police force—the town becomes the trooper's responsibility, 24/7. Taking patrol this evening rather than calling in for coverage gave me a feel for what goes on when I'm usually off duty."

"Well, that'll sure change when the summer residents head back here," Gaby remarked. "Woodson Falls has a totally different feel then."

"How's that?"

"The lake attracts a lot of visitors, mostly good people, families. But like anywhere, there are always a few troublemakers. Party too hard, drink too much, don't leave when the park closes. A few break-ins, robberies. Small stuff. Some shoplifting."

"Lived here long?"

"Just a couple of years, though I spent summers here when I was a kid. I lived in New York City before that."

"Big change. I know. I moved up here from the Bronx just a short time ago. Here's the tow truck we've been waiting for."

The driver from Teddy's Garage in Prescott lost little time in loading Gaby's car onto his flat-bed trailer. He took her phone number and promised to call the next day after they'd had time to estimate what repairs might be needed. After he left, Gaby and the trooper returned to his cruiser.

"Well, thanks, Officer Thomas… or is it Trooper Thomas? I'd probably still be standing in the road—frozen solid—if you hadn't happened along."

"It's Officer Thomas, and I'm happy to help. Where can I take you? Home, I'm sure, unless you'd like to join me for supper. I'm just coming off duty, and you look like you could use a hot meal."

"A hot meal would be nice."

And so, Gaby found herself back where her day began, in a booth at the Sunshine Café, this time with a weary Officer Thomas sitting across from her, reflecting her own fatigue in his drooping eyes and the shadow of his beard, which had passed five o'clock hours ago.

"What made you think I was new at this?" Gaby asked, glancing over the herbal tea she was sipping. She held the cup in both hands to relieve the numbing chill that seemed to have permeated her entire body.

"Huh?"

"At the police station. When you came over to ask if I was there to see Walter Murphy."

"Oh, that. Yeah. Most lawyers start to throw their weight around as soon as they get to the station. Act as if they own the place. You said 'please.' Big difference," he answered after wolfing down a piece of the meatloaf he had ordered.

"Well, you were right. I have never dealt with a situation like Walter's," she responded, biting into her grilled cheese sandwich while her tomato soup cooled.

"If you don't do criminal law, what kind of law do you practice?"

"Mostly wills, trusts, probate, with a smattering of real estate and a bit of nonprofit incorporation every now and then. Just 'small country lawyer' kinds of things," she replied. "Right now, I'm working on an estate the probate court asked me to take on. Up in Woodson Lake Estates."

"Interesting?"

"More puzzling than anything, but I haven't really dug into it yet. So, what brought you to this corner of Connecticut? It seems an odd choice for someone from the Bronx."

"I like to hike and hunt. Sometimes fish," he answered after swallowing a clump of mashed potatoes. "I left the NYPD and New York when I had enough service years to retire with a decent pension. Plus, I was sick of the corruption, the violence that pervaded my work. You? Don't you miss the challenge of being a New York attorney?"

"I hold a New York license, but I never practiced there. I left the city a few years ago, right after I finished law school. I needed to start fresh, but I also wanted something familiar. Woodson Falls seemed to be waiting for me."

"Start fresh? What did you do before you became a lawyer?"

"Taught philosophy at Columbia University, following in my parents' footsteps. They both teach philosophy at Wesleyan. But after a few years of teaching philosophical principles to mostly bored sophomores and juniors who were filling a humanities requirement, I started to get just as bored as they were and knew I needed a change. The law promised a degree of relative precision and finality, different than the sometimes opaque pursuit of lofty ideals. Something I could get my arms around."

"Is it what you expected?"

"Mostly. It's interesting—and different, but sometimes the law can be as murky as Socrates. So, what made you go into law enforcement?"

The trooper mopped up a bit of gravy with the last piece of his roll, then looked up. "My dad was a cop, and his father before him. I was an MP in the military, so it was a natural transition to the police force. And it was okay for a long, long time. I served mostly in the 75th Precinct, in Brooklyn. It's a pretty rough and dangerous place, even after my experiences in Iraq and Afghanistan. But I liked the challenge and was promoted to detective early. Even got my sergeant's stripes the year before I retired."

"So, if you retired from the police department in New York, why did you become a state trooper?"

Pushing his empty plate to the side and picking up his coffee cup, he said, "It gets in your blood, police work does. You begin to crave the action, the people, the connections that policing entails, although not much seems to be happening around here. Still, the work is familiar and keeps me from turning into myself, becoming too insular."

"Same for me. It's easy to retreat into a comfortable corner and forget the world, but that gets old pretty fast."

Gaby finished her soup, then looked up. "You look as tired as I feel. Have far to go to get home?"

"I have a place up near the police barracks in Litchfield, but I'll probably bunk down at the firehouse tonight, given the ice storm. That'll give me an early start in the morning. I've been spending a lot of time trying to get to know the town officials, the businessmen. Get a feel for the town."

"It's a nice, mostly quiet place to live. People here tend to keep to themselves, though they're friendly enough."

They sat in silence until the waitress brought the check.

"Let me," Gaby said, reaching for the check.

"No, it's on me." He threw some bills onto the table. "Let's get you home."

# Chapter 10

"TELL ME YOUR STORY, MR. PIETER JORGENSON, SO I CAN MAKE some sense of your estate," Gaby murmured. She propped the wooden figure she had found at the Lakeview Terrace house against her desk lamp and emptied her briefcase of the files she had collected.

*Hard to believe that was just yesterday.*

She added the accumulated mail and copies of the paperwork she had retrieved from Town Hall to the pile on her desk. She could hear the bell-like tinkling of ice as it cracked and fell from tree limbs. Last night's storm had encased the tree branches in ice, creating a sparkling fairyland that was quickly dissolving in the morning sun that streamed through her office window.

Sipping her second cup of breakfast coffee, she considered how she would approach administering the estate. It was tempting to dive right in and pick out the details needed for the probate paperwork, but experience had taught her that doing so inevitably resulted in missing something important that she'd have to search for later. It was wiser to examine each item on her desk to determine what, if any, relevance it might have for administering the estate.

Gaby pulled a fresh legal pad from her desk drawer. Beginning with the information from the town records, she jotted down the approximate fair market value of the Lakeview Terrace property based on the assessor's records, which would be the first item on the required inventory of assets. According to the tax records, the two vehicles registered to Jorgenson—the Jeep she had spotted in the garage and the Ford pickup—were collectively valued at about $6,000. Jorgenson probably had driven the truck to New York, where he had died unexpectedly. Gaby would need to contact the New York police to determine where the truck was being stored.

The ring of the telephone interrupted her thoughts.

"Law offices. Gabriella Quinn speaking," she announced to the caller.

"Oh, Gaby! Fran here. I just wanted to thank you for all you did for Walter yesterday. I tried to call last evening after he got home and told me what happened, but you didn't pick up. I wanted to be sure you knew how grateful we both are to you for taking care of the situation."

"My pleasure, Fran. I'm just glad Walter wasn't in any trouble. Crazy that it turned out to be a case of mistaken identity. Who would have thought?"

"Exactly," Fran exclaimed. "But it was your mentioning having seen Walter at the restaurant yesterday morning that really did the trick. What a break!"

"Just happy everything worked out."

"What do I owe you, Gaby? You spent hours with Walter yesterday."

"No charge, Fran. We're friends."

"But… Gaby, your time is valuable. Please let me pay you."

"Really, Fran. No. I'm just grateful I could help."

"Okay, if you insist. Have a great day, Gaby. And again, thanks so very much—from both of us."

"No problem, Fran. See you in church Sunday," Gaby replied, hanging up the phone and returning to her work.

*Where was I? Contact the police about the truck*—"Oh, my goodness! More important, where did his body end up and where was he buried?"

She re-examined the death certificate. There were lots of blank spaces. Paul Evans, Jorgenson's Connecticut attorney, was the informant for what little information appeared on the form. She'd need to speak with Evans to see if he had more information about Jorgenson than had been requested by the medical examiner issuing the death certificate. But where was Jorgenson buried, and who paid for the funeral?

Gaby recalled reading a *New York Times* exposé several years ago about the management of unclaimed bodies in New York City. A mere forty-eight hours were given for next-of-kin to claim the body. If no one came forward, the deceased person was listed as a potential medical school cadaver or buried on Hart Island, New York City's potter's field. And the roster of deceased persons passing through a morgue was kept private, which didn't allow next-of-kin to search for missing loved ones. The uproar that followed had led to legislation requiring morgues to engage in a thorough search for relatives using all available resources. She would contact the medical examiner to determine which morgue had handled Jorgenson's body and whether they'd been able to locate any next-of-kin.

The phone rang again.

"Law—"

"Ms. Quinn? Dave, down at Teddy's Garage. The repairs to your Subaru are going to run several thousand dollars. Did you call your insurer?"

"First thing this morning."

"The work should be covered, except for the deductible, of course. Problem is it'll take at least a week to get the parts and do the work. I imagine you'll need a loaner?"

"Absolutely."

"We lined one up for you, just in case, but I can't get it up to you until late this afternoon. Will that be a problem?"

"No. I didn't plan to be out and about today. The afternoon will be fine."

"Good. With the ice storm last night, we've got our hands full with busted fenders and wrecks."

"I can only imagine. Thanks for the call."

"Someone will be by late this afternoon, probably around four or five. That okay?"

"That's fine. Have a good day."

"You, too, Ms. Quinn."

Returning to her work, Gaby recalled Rusty saying there was a lot of interesting stuff on the second level of the house, so she'd need to return there to take a look at the contents to guesstimate its value for the inventory.

*I wonder if it'll be worth having an estate sale, which would be difficult in that location. Maybe I should just sell the contents of the house to a company that will remove everything for disposal or resale. Guess I'll have to wait to see what's there.*

She added to the growing list on the legal pad the places she had failed to explore when she was first in the house—the kitchen cabinets and refrigerator, the garage and its Jeep—in addition to the other two lower levels of the house. Also, the large boxes in the second bedroom and the dresser drawers they had been blocking. Lots of work. She wasn't likely to find much, but you never knew. Anyway, it was all part of the job.

Gaby removed the rubber band from the pile of Jorgenson's mail she had picked up at the post office and began sorting through it, discarding the junk mail and setting aside the pile of magazines and catalogs in case some mail had slipped between the pages. She opened the first-class mail as she came across it: electric and telephone bills, a bill from a heating oil company, several letters from Attorney Evans as well as notices from the court, and a bank statement.

The phone rang again.

"Law offices. Gabriella Quinn…"

"Gaby! Hi! It's Nell! Haven't seen you in ages! What's up? You okay?"

"Hi, Nell. How are you?" Gaby responded.

One of Gaby's closest friends, Nellwyn Whitney seemed always to speak in exclamation points. She had retired from a lucrative law practice in New York City to pursue her interest in herbs and crystals, eventually opening Rainbows & Unicorns, a small shop located next to Woodson Falls' hardware store. Nell carried an ever-changing array of goods ranging from precious stones, crystals and jewelry to teas, Native American dream catchers, herbs and New Age healing items. Figures of unicorns peeked out from the shelves and hung from the ceiling. Her positive energy and warm, inviting manner attracted a broad following.

Gaby had visited the shop often when she first moved to Woodson Falls. Back then, she was still suffering from frequent panic attacks connected to the assault that had killed Joe and left her wounded in both body and spirit. The calming atmosphere Nell had created allowed Gaby to relax a bit, and she eventually shared her experiences with the lingering effects of the PTSD she suffered. It was Nell who had suggested that Gaby look into getting an emotional support animal, which had led her to acquire Katrina. The dog had gotten her through some rocky moments, which fortunately arose less and less frequently now.

"Just got back from a gem show in New York!" Nell exclaimed. "Bought too much as usual, but I'll eventually find a place for everything. What've you been up to?"

"Judge Taylor asked me to take on an estate. I've been plowing through the information I've collected," Gaby responded, leafing through the magazines and catalogs. "Now this is interesting. Why would someone who subscribes to *This Old House, Car and Driver, Fine Woodworking* and *Popular Science* be getting catalogs from medical supply companies? May not be important, but who knows. Might fit in somehow."

"I guess you'll have to wait and see. Have any time for breakfast some morning this week? We should catch up. And you can fill me in on anything else you come across."

"That'd be great. Where and when? I'm pretty free these days."

"How about the Greene Bean, Tuesday, about eight? I have to open the shop by eleven, but I need to pick up some things in Prescott first."

"Works for me," Gaby replied. "See you then."

"Bye now! Gotta hang up! A customer just came in."

Setting the mail aside, Gaby dove back into the accumulated files, working through them systematically and making notes as she went. Despite the day being punctuated by several more telephone calls, she had made her way to the bottom of the piles of materials by late afternoon, her legal pad now containing three pages of notes that would guide her further work on the estate.

"C'mon, Kat," she called, pulling on her down vest and donning her woolen beanie. "Time for a run."

# Chapter 11

WHILE SHE WAS JOGGING, GABY MENTALLY REVIEWED WHAT SHE had learned from the files she had recovered at Jorgenson's house.

The bank statement in Jorgenson's mail revealed a substantial sum of money in an account owned jointly with a Sofia Jorgenson, who turned out to be his mother. Based on the materials in the files, Gaby figured out that Jorgenson had lived with her in the Bronx until the house in Woodson Lake Estates was habitable. When his mother became ill, she sold the two-family house and moved to Connecticut to live with her son until her death about nine months ago. The calendar Gaby found hanging in Jorgenson's locker was from the previous year and noted the date his mother was admitted to the hospital and her date of death, a mere ten days later. Jorgenson's ties to the Bronx explained the many New York phone numbers and addresses that appeared in the small address book she had found in the dresser in his bedroom.

The proceeds of the sale of the Bronx property most likely accounted for the sizeable bank account, although Gaby imagined some of the money was used to pay off the construction mortgage. Three CDs and a savings account totaled about $150,000. Jorgenson or his mother must have had other funds to support acquiring the land in Woodson Lake Estates. Once Gaby received the official decree from the probate court appointing her as the administrator of Jorgenson's estate, she would convert the bank accounts to estate accounts, giving her access to funds to pay any accumulated bills and other expenses related to administering the estate.

Bank statements indicated that several bills were paid automatically through the savings account. The mother's social security checks that had been deposited into the account monthly stopped with her death. Automatic weekly deposits of $375 continued to be made as of the most recent bank statement, payments to Jorgenson from a successful worker's compensation action. Rusty was right. Jorgenson had been a roofer, suffering multiple fractures in a fall while working for Kings Roofing in Yonkers, New York. His injuries left him unable to return to work as a roofer, but he had applied his skills as a carpenter in doing odd jobs in and around New York City, which were recorded in the notebook she had found in his locker.

Jorgenson's address book listed two uncles—Lucas and Oscar—no last names. There was nothing in the files about Jorgenson's father. Gaby was uncertain whether he had died some time ago and whether the "uncles" were Sofia's brothers and possible heirs to Jorgenson's estate, brothers-in-law, or male friends Jorgenson was taught to address as "Uncle." According to the calendar, Oscar had died a few months after Sofia. Gaby planned to call Lucas, hoping he was a blood relative of Jorgenson or could provide some insight into potential beneficiaries of the estate.

There was extensive correspondence with attorneys related to an unsuccessful suit Jorgenson had filed against Norman Lutz, the developer of Woodson Lake Estates, who Frank had mentioned when they talked at his store. Jorgenson claimed that road drainage was flowing across his property because a culvert designed to direct drainage away from downhill lots had collapsed. Gaby had come across a few sketches of the Lakeview Terrace house showing the area of the foundation affected by the drainage. Apparently, Lutz had refused to do anything about the situation, countersuing that Jorgenson had created his own problems by blocking the culvert with a rock.

*Guess when he lost the suit against Lutz, Jorgenson looked to his neighbor, Loomis, for a financial award to fund a solution to the problem.*

Gaby was intrigued by the claims and counterclaims evident in the correspondence and could see both sides of the issue. After all, that's what law school taught aspiring attorneys: how to see both sides of an issue so you could be prepared to effectively rebut your opponent's arguments. Still, all of this had little to do with administering this estate, so she had put the letters back in the appropriate file and moved on.

The yellow pages torn from the phone book suggested that Jorgenson was looking for someone to install a septic and dig a well, so it was likely the house still lacked both and hadn't been issued a Certificate of Occupancy. Gaby would have to verify this with the building and health departments at Town Hall, but guessed that the many empty plastic bottles she had seen in the house served as Jorgenson's water source, with sewage directed down the hillside toward the lake—not unusual in rural areas, but still in violation of the health code. She didn't fancy getting involved with having the necessary well and septic work done while the estate was in administration, so the house would have to be sold to someone willing to do the work, lessening its value to the estate.

And that was all Gaby had discovered that related in any way to the management of the estate.

Turning to head back home, Gaby chuckled as she recalled the unsigned, handwritten letter she had found among Jorgenson's papers. It read:

Dear neighbor,
Please do not take my little doggy away.
She is a nice little doggy and we love
her and she loves me.

*Fifi wants me to tell you that first-grade classes are now open for spelling.*

Gaby had noticed the many misspelled words and poor grammar evident in Jorgenson's handwritten drafts of letters to various attorneys and couldn't help but agree with Angela Markham's assessment.

Trailed by her dog, Kat, Gaby continued her run toward home and thought about what hadn't made sense. The small box of snapshots she had found in the bedroom dresser contained about a dozen photos of street scenes. While she hadn't recognized the places, she felt certain the photos had been taken in and around New York City. *Maybe Nell will recognize the locations. I'll bring the box of photos with me when we meet next Tuesday.*

The reverse side of each of the photos had been marked in pencil with a date, the initials BX, BK, M or Q, and a number 1 through 5. Based on these markings, the photos could be arranged into five piles. *Probably different shots of the same location,* she imagined. Similar notations appeared on the calendar, corresponding to the dates on the snapshots. While other entries on the calendar made sense as reminders of events, such as his mother's hospitalization and subsequent death, these cryptic notes remained puzzling, and Gaby wondered whether they would eventually provide some insight that might assist in estate administration.

She hoped the phone calls she planned to make on Monday—to the medical examiner to determine the disposition of Jorgenson's body, the police to locate his truck, and Jorgenson's Uncle Lucas to identify next-of-kin and anything else of relevance to her work on the estate—would help to flesh out the information she had gathered. Along with work to be done on other matters that required her attention and her intent to spend more time at the Lakeview Terrace house, she had several full days planned. Plus, she had promised to make brownies for Saturday evening's dinner with Sally and the kids.

# Chapter 12

"SPRINGER, EVANS, STRAUSS AND GERKIN. HOW MAY I DIRECT your call?" announced the receptionist at Paul Evans' law firm. Gaby had decided to begin her search for her dead client's body and pickup truck by talking to the attorney police had contacted after finding Jorgenson. Knowing something about the circumstances surrounding his death and the discovery of his body seemed as good a place to start as any.

"Attorney Gabriella Quinn calling. I'd like to speak with Attorney Evans, please, if he's available."

"Let me put you through. Have a good day."

"Thank you," Gaby responded, pulling a fresh legal pad closer as she waited for Evans to come on the line.

Still tired from her long day at the police station with Walter and the ice storm Thursday night, Gaby had decided to take this past weekend off. There was seldom any real urgency attached to her law work, one of the benefits of a practice focused primarily on wills, trusts and estate administration. Yes, there were deadlines for certain filings, but there were also long periods of enforced waiting, particularly during the five months allowed for creditors to present their bills for payment by an estate. She felt refreshed having been away from her desk for a while and was ready to plunge back into her work.

"Paul Evans here. Can I help you?"

"Good morning, Attorney Evans. Gabriella Quinn. I'm the attorney appointed by the probate court to administer Pieter Jorgenson's estate. I understand that you were representing Jorgenson at the time he died, and I was wondering—"

"Ah, yeah. Bill Harrison said you might call. Great weather we're having, don't you think? It's been a hard winter, but spring is finally in the air!"

"So true. Saw my first robin this morning. Bill mentioned that the New York police contacted you after finding your business card in Jorgenson's wallet. Could you tell me anything about where he died or anything about Jorgenson? I need to get to the right people to learn the disposition of his body and where the truck he drove into the city might be stored, and I'm searching for next-of-kin."

"Didn't have all that much to tell the police when they called, and I haven't learned any more since."

"Anything you can tell me would be a help," Gaby said. "I don't mind doing the leg work, but I do need to know what direction to go in."

"I hear you. Well, his truck was found down near the Village. Some kids told the beat cop down there that a man was slumped over the driver's wheel of a pickup truck and that he hadn't moved in some time. The beat cop went to the scene and discovered Jorgenson dead. Manhattan South detectives took it from there. They're the ones who called me. Apparently, no foul play was suspected, but they were exploring any possibilities, including the reason Jorgenson might have been in the area.

"I didn't have much to tell them," Evans continued. "I knew Jorgenson did odd jobs as a carpenter both in Connecticut and New York. That he lived alone with his mother. That they had moved up here from the Bronx a year or two ago and that she died sometime last year. Jorgenson never spoke of family, but then again, he didn't talk much. Very angry guy. Kept railing against the developer of

Woodson Lake Estates as well as his neighbor. Talked about some secret that was supposed to win the case for us, but never told me what that 'secret' was. Whole thing was about road drainage flowing onto his property, which he blamed on the developer and then on his neighbor. We ended up settling the case after he didn't make the court appearance. The whole easement issue is still pending. The settlement required Jorgenson to grant the easement to Loomis for a fair price, but nothing has been negotiated to my knowledge."

"Yeah, Bill told me a bit about the case. So, nothing more about what Jorgenson might have been doing in New York, other than the possibility of pursuing an odd job?"

"I didn't talk to the guy much after the suit was filed. You know, these things take time to make their way through the courts. Jorgenson questioned every penny on my billings, but didn't seem to mind taking up my time with his rants. You know how it is. Clients never seem to think that billable hours apply to them when they want to let off steam. I let sleeping dogs lie rather than rattle that lion's cage, so most of my communications with Jorgenson were through the mail."

Gaby smiled to herself over Evans' mixed metaphor but said, "Hmm… Yes, I've heard from his neighbors that he could be a pretty difficult character. Well, thanks for your time. I appreciate your pointing me toward Manhattan South. I'll take it from there."

"Good luck to you. We'll be filing a claim for unpaid time spent on the case. Can I have it sent to your attention?"

"Of course," Gaby said, before thanking Evans again and hanging up.

*Next stop, the medical examiner.* The M.E.'s name appeared on the death certificate and it was relatively easy to find the phone number for the M.E.'s office online. A clerk answered the phone.

"Office of the Chief Medical Examiner. How can I help you?"

"Good morning. My name is Gabriella Quinn. I'm an attorney in Connecticut trying to determine the disposition of the body of a Connecticut resident who died suddenly in Manhattan. The medical examiner issuing the death certificate was a Dr. Michael Garrity. Can you connect me to his office?"

"I can, but no one is going to help you over the phone, honey. This office protects the identity of the dead folks we deal with. You'll need to come down to the office in person with proper authorization before any information can be released about one of the decedents we handled—if we handled the person you're looking for."

"I just want to know if this is the right place. Does Dr. Garrity work here?" Gaby asked.

"I just can't provide that information," the operator insisted.

"You mean I can't even—"

"I mean no information without you presenting the proper authorization."

"Well, thank you anyway. Have a nice day," Gaby said, hanging up the phone and shaking her head. *This is going to be harder than I thought.*

She had received the court decree appointing her as the administrator of Jorgenson's estate in the mail, along with several probate certificates for managing his property. Similar paperwork was referred to as "letters testamentary" in New York, and she assumed that was what was needed to open the door to the M.E.'s office. It would take a trip to New York City to get the simple information she was looking for unless she could find it some other way.

She had jotted down the phone numbers for the two precincts covering Greenwich Village while she was online, picked one, and called them next. The operator who answered the call transferred her to the traffic division where the person manning the phone responded to her inquiry by asking her to hold the line. After Gaby listened to crackly background music for five minutes, he came back to the phone.

"Hello? Ms. Quinn? Any vehicle found in Manhattan under the circumstances you described would be held in the impound lot with instructions not to put it up for auction until a representative of the person's estate filed a claim for it and paid the necessary fees. The impound lot is located at Pier 76 off the West Side Highway. I suggest calling them for more information. The number's 212-869-2929."

"Thank you! You've been most helpful," Gaby said, reflecting that it was easier to locate a vehicle than a body. *Crazy*, she thought, dialing the number.

"Manhattan Impound, Tony speaking."

Gaby explained what she was looking for, giving a description of the truck, its tag number and VIN, as well as the approximate date the truck would have been brought to the impound.

"Hey, listen, lady. I can't be trotting around this place looking for your truck. There are thousands of vehicles here. You'll have to come here with the title to the truck, the death certificate for the owner, something authorizing you to claim the vehicle, as well as your own identification. And you better bring a certified check. The fees to release the vehicle will run well over $600."

"What! Can't any fees be waived in a case like this?

"No can do, lady. It's a basic $150 impound fee plus $15 per day for storage. So, I recommend getting here as soon as you can."

"You've got to have some system for locating impounded vehicles," Gaby pressed. "Can you just tell me if the truck is there?"

"No way, no how. We'll know when you get here. And you'll probably want to arrange for transportation, too. No telling what shape that truck might be in after sitting here for close to a month. Oh, and you'll need a release from the traffic division."

"Well, thanks," Gaby said, hanging up. *For nothing*. She hoped her next call, to the Uncle Lucas listed in Jorgenson's address book, would get her somewhere. She had verified that Uncle Lucas was Lucas Jorgenson using an online reverse telephone directory, giving her a bit more comfort in making this cold call. Lucas answered the phone on the third ring.

"Hello?"

"Mr. Jorgenson? My name is Gabriella Quinn. I'm an attorney in Connecticut. I believe you're related to a Pieter Jorgenson?"

"What's that idiot gone and done now? I'm done cleaning up that imbecile's messes. No more! You his lawyer? Can't pay you. Got my own problems, you know."

"Excuse me? No, no. Oh, dear. I'm sorry to say that Pieter died recently while in New York. Hadn't you been notified?

"He died? He was much too young to just die! What'd he do to get himself killed?"

"Nothing, apparently. Seems he died of natural causes. I've been appointed by the Connecticut probate court to manage his estate, and I'm trying to identify any next-of-kin."

"Died, humph. Died. Well, imagine that. Died. What do you need to know?"

"Was Pieter married? Did he have any children, siblings? Any information you can provide would help."

"Never married. No children, at least not that I know anything about. He was a bastard—in both senses of that word. My sister, Sofie—God rest her soul—never got married. She was a looker and a pushover, especially when it came to men. No telling who Pieter's father was. Sofie raised that boy on her own. She tried, tried real hard, but she never could control him.

"Pieter was small for his age when he was young, and what you'd call 'slow.' Constantly bullied by the kids at his school. When he finally got his growth—in his teens, I think—he was big enough to intimidate grown men. Got involved with a gang and ended up getting into all kinds of trouble. Got caught breaking into cars, although he wasn't arrested, thank goodness. That would have killed Sofie.

"Like I said, Pieter wasn't too bright. Always looking for the next best thing."

"And you're Pieter's uncle? Sofia's brother?"

"Yup. Just the three of us—my older brother Oscar, Sofie in the middle, and me. I'm the youngest and the only one left. Does that make me Pieter's next-of-kin? Can't have had much. I know they both lived on a shoestring."

"Actually, I'm not certain at this point just who will inherit whatever is in the estate." While Gaby knew Lucas was the most likely beneficiary of Jorgenson's estate based on Connecticut's law of intestacy, which determined beneficiaries of a decedent who didn't have a will, she hesitated to say so as someone else might emerge as a closer relative or she might find a will that indicated the beneficiaries of Jorgenson's estate. "Are there any cousins?"

"Well, my wife and I have two girls, Sonia and Sylvia, and Oscar left one girl, Brianna. Sofie's boy was the only one who would have carried on the Jorgenson name, that is if he had had any children. Guess it's the end of the line for us Jorgenson's."

"So sorry to be the bearer of bad news. Could you give me contact information for your daughters and for Brianna, and any other relatives? The probate court here in Connecticut needs the information just in case there's anything in the estate."

Lucas gave Gaby the information then said, "Where's he buried? He probably would've wanted to be buried with Sofie. For all the pain in the butt he was, he loved Sofie. They were real close."

"If you and your daughters and niece are the only next of kin and hadn't heard about his death, then it's likely Pieter's body is still being held in the New York morgue." Gaby thought it best not to speculate on Jorgenson's possible burial on Hart Island or the donation of his body to a medical school. "When I find out the details, I'll get back in touch with you."

"I don't have much money for a burial and all," Lucas was quick to say.

"The estate would be responsible for burial costs," Gaby told him. "By the way, Mr. Jorgenson," she continued, "do you happen to know whether Pieter had a will?"

"I would doubt it. He wasn't the type to plan for the future. Neither was Sofie."

"Given that, even though you live in New York, I know the probate court would consider appointing you to manage Pieter's estate since it seems you're his closest relative. Would you like me to request the probate court make such an appointment?"

"No way, no how. I've got enough business of my own without having to get involved with Pieter's affairs."

"That's fine. I'll keep you informed as things proceed, and I know you'll be getting periodic notices from the probate court along the way. I'll call you again with information on how to claim your nephew's body and arrange for transportation to Connecticut, if that's where he'll be buried. In the meantime, here's my contact information in case you have any questions." Giving Lucas her cell and office numbers, Gaby expressed her condolences again and ended the call.

*Well, that was interesting.*

"Next stop, New York, I guess," Gaby murmured, cringing at the thought of a trip to the city. After finishing law school, Gaby had studiously avoided returning to New York, where memories of her life with Joe were likely to deal an emotional blow she wasn't sure she could bear.

# Chapter 13

SPRING HAD SLIPPED IN OVER THE WEEKEND, SUNSHINE SPREAD-ing its warmth across Woodson Falls. The new season's smells seemed particularly sweet this year—the gentle fragrance of some prolific shrub, the musty smell of damp earth, the fresh tang of the lake.

As the sun set Monday evening, Gaby had noticed the geese, flying in reverse formation, returning home, and had fallen asleep to the chorus of peepers cheeping down by the pond.

After her morning run with Kat, Gaby headed to Prescott for breakfast with Nell. She was eager to see her friend as well as to ask for her help in planning the trip to New York to claim Jorgenson's body and arrange for the disposal of his truck. *Maybe I can get her to come with me. That would be better than tackling this alone.*

She had packed up the small box of photographs from Jorgenson's bedroom. She hoped Nell might recognize some of the places, tying up that loose end, which might even lead somewhere.

It was hard for Gaby to imagine Nell in a New York City court-room, prim and proper in the two-piece suit and low heels that were practically *de rigour* for female attorneys. Once in Woodson Falls, Nell had indulged her passion for purple, dressing in long and flowing gauzy caftans and scarfs, her short brown hair threaded with silver, flitting about like a hummingbird and just as tiny. Early in their friendship, Gaby had felt like a horse beside the petite Nell despite her own slender five-foot-six frame.

Nell had left a thriving practice as a prominent personal injury attorney who had attracted cases with high visibility and equally high insurance settlements or, if the case went to trial, even higher jury awards. She had been more than willing to serve as a mentor to Gaby when she began her practice in Woodson Falls, something every beginning attorney needed, especially one who—like Gaby—had decided on a solo practice. Nell had a knack for pulling together seemingly unrelated facts, creating a possible picture of past events that eventually proved accurate nearly all of the time. Her experience coupled with her intuitive sensitivities enabled her to ask the right questions as well as follow her hunches to uncover the essence of a case. Gaby's friendship with Nell had helped her to nurture her own intuition, which had proved useful in solving the riddles that law cases sometimes presented.

As soon as Gaby entered the Greene Bean, Nell jumped up from her seat to greet her with a big hug. "Boy, it's great to see you, Gaby!"

"Great to see you, too, Nell. Too much time between visits. Tell me all about your trip to New York. Everything you hoped for?"

After describing some of her finds at the recent gem show and her plans to reorganize her already packed shop to accommodate her latest purchases, Nell said, "So, tell me about this case Bud Taylor sent your way! An estate?"

"Uh-huh," Gaby mumbled, finishing a bite of the lemon ginger scone she had ordered for breakfast. "Up in Woodson Lake Estates. Guy—Jorgenson—died in New York, although it's still unclear what he was doing there. He worked at the school as a crossing guard and apparently the kids liked him. Sally Gorman's son, Ryan, told me he stood up for kids who were bullied by other students. On the other hand, a neighbor of his I spoke with sure didn't like him and said that none of his neighbors did.

"It's like he was two people. One made birdhouses that were sold at the hardware store and gave snack packs of animal crackers to kids at school. The other was a man most of his neighbors avoided. Regardless of whether they liked him or not, people knew little to nothing about him.

"I've been able to track down an uncle and three cousins as the only next-of-kin. There's money there, both in the value of the house and in bank accounts, and no apparent debt that I've found yet. I haven't finished looking through the house, so there may be tangible property of value too. It's just that there are these odd things I turn up that make no sense and probably mean nothing, but…"

"But you feel you need to pull on those threads to see where they lead. I know what you mean, but it's the nature of the beast. A lawyer is trained to go down all those blind alleys to eliminate them from consideration. If you don't…"

"I know. One of those loose ends can pop up and bite you. It's all just so tedious. And made harder, I think, by knowing next to nothing about the man. It's different than handling the estate of a client you've gotten to know over time. Then the little things tend to make more sense, and it's easier to make your way through the weeds. With this guy, all I have to go on is this gut feeling that there's more there than meets the eye."

"Like the medical supply catalogs amidst the magazines?"

Gaby laughed. "You remembered. And these," she continued, pulling the small box of photographs from her purse. "They're just pictures of street scenes, possibly in New York City, but I'm not sure. I was hoping you might recognize one or more of the places."

"These are clearly New York City locations, but not your usual tourist attractions. I can't place all of them, but this one looks vaguely familiar," Nell said, her manicured nail tapping the photo of a fence bordering a body of water, decorated with large metal figures of fish. "Let me look closer. There's a small sign here, just to the right of the young girl," she continued, pulling out an antique magnifying glass from a side pocket of her commodious purse. "Yes! The sign says 'Tautog,' which I recall thinking was an odd name for a fish. Let me think."

Gaby pointed to the penciled notations on the backs of the photos, some of which depicted playgrounds and others, storefronts. "Do these jog your memory?" she asked Nell.

"Of course! BK must stand for Brooklyn! This snapshot must have been taken at Bensonhurst Park! Not the nicest park in the city, but it's on the water and has a decent playground, ball fields. I remember being surprised those metal fish weren't covered with graffiti!" Nell shuffled through the rest of the photographs. Another labeled BK was of a basketball court, where some young kids were tossing a battered ball into a hoop bare of any semblance of a basket. "Yes, I'm sure. These two are of Bensonhurst Park. The others were definitely taken in New York, but I can't make out any signage or a familiar building. Still, the notations obviously refer to four of the five boroughs: BK for Brooklyn, BX for the Bronx, Q for Queens, and M for Manhattan. None of Staten Island. Interesting. What else have you unearthed?"

"I didn't bring it with me, but I found a carved wooden figure of a man that was lying on a workbench when I first entered the house. Lots of detail, and I'm assuming it's intended to be a self-portrait of a sort. The figure had a small gadget that Rusty Dolan thought was an old roofing tool. Turned out that Jorgenson had been a roofer. He was collecting workers' compensation after a bad fall."

"Hmm… Anything else?"

"There were some smaller wooden figures that looked like they could be children, both boys and girls. I thought at first they might represent Jorgenson's kids when they were small, or possibly cousins. But according to his uncle, Jorgenson had no children, only cousins—all girls—so I'm not sure if those figures mean anything or not. He was a skilled craftsman. The birdhouses he was making were professional quality, and Frank told me he sold quite a few at the hardware store."

Nell smiled across the table at her friend. "You certainly have developed an eye for detail," she said. "Finely tuned observation skills can be a great help in dealing with a case like this, and it looks like you're enjoying the quest!"

"To a point. I need to get back to the house to go through the lower level, which Rusty said was filled with 'interesting' stuff. And I need to take a trip to New York to determine the disposition of Jorgenson's body and claim the pickup truck he drove there."

"I know that's going to be hard for you," Nell said with a sad smile. "Wish I could go with you, but with the store…"

"Of course not! I wouldn't think of asking," Gaby replied, struggling to hide her disappointment from her friend, who she had hoped would offer to make the trip with her. "I just got such a runaround when I tried to call a few places—just to expedite the trip, so I know where to go. I dread hitting a lot of dead ends and having to spend more time in the city than absolutely necessary. Everyone seemed so close-mouthed about simple questions, and I didn't even bother trying to determine what the detectives at Manhattan South who investigated Jorgenson's death had learned."

"Have you met our new resident state trooper? Matt Thomas? He's been introducing himself to the merchants in town, and we had a long chat last week. He recently retired from the NYPD. Maybe he'd be willing to help open a few doors for you, make a few calls. Seemed like a nice enough fellow."

"We've met, though not in the best of circumstances," Gaby said, describing her encounter with the trooper at the Prescott police station followed by his rescuing her when she was stranded on the road during the recent ice storm.

"I don't know if I'd be comfortable asking for his help," she continued. "I know he's just getting started here and trying to get a feel for the town."

"Gaby," Nell replied. "You never know until you try."

# Chapter 14

IT WAS SUNNY AND BRIGHT WHEN GABY LEFT PRESCOTT, A COOL breeze blowing away winter, freshening the air. The resident state trooper's cruiser was parked outside the Woodson Falls Fire Department where his office was located, so Gaby made the split-second decision to pull into the parking lot.

*It's now or never.* She gritted her teeth and pushed open the door to the building. *He can always say "no."*

Gaby still wished Nell could have come with her to the city. She wasn't sure she could handle the trip on her own. *Here goes.*

Peeking around the trooper's office door, Gaby saw that he was engrossed in paperwork. She hesitated for a moment then knocked softly.

Looking up, the trooper said, "Ms. Quinn! That you?"

"Officer Thomas?"

"Matt, please. What can I do for you? Did you get your car back yet?"

"No. It's still in the shop. I'm driving a loaner at least until the end of the week, possibly longer. By the way, thank you again for rescuing me the other night and for dinner."

"No problem. Happy to serve. Can I help you with anything?"

"I just came from breakfast with Nellwyn Whitney. She owns Rainbows & Unicorns here in town. She suggested I talk to you."

"Ah, yes. Nell Whitney. We had a nice chat the other day. Interesting person. Even more interesting store," he said, gesturing to the chair in front of the desk. "Have a seat. What do you need?"

"It's about the estate I'm handling up in Woodson Lake Estates," Gaby said, sitting at the edge of the chair, poised to leave as quickly as possible if the trooper said he couldn't help her. "The individual in question died in New York. I'm trying to determine where his body and the truck he drove into the city are located. I've been getting the runaround with practically every call I've made so far. Obviously, I'll need to make a trip into the city. I just don't know where to start, where to go, who to ask for. Nell thought you might be able to point me in the right direction, perhaps make some calls so I'm not running around in circles while I'm there."

"I can make a few calls for you. It's not that long since I left the NYPD. I still have buddies there. What's the dead guy's name?"

"Pieter Jorgenson," Gaby replied, spelling out the first and last names. "Died back in January, apparently of natural causes. In his fifties." She paused. "Used to live in the Bronx," she added, wondering why she was giving the trooper that bit of extraneous information.

"Any idea where he was found?"

"Down in the Village."

"Manhattan South, most likely the Sixth Precinct. Possibly the Ninth. Did you try either of those?"

"I think I spoke with someone in the Ninth Precinct. I never thought about the possibility another precinct might be involved. In any event, the person I spoke with was the most helpful. I didn't expect someone to reveal anything about the case over the phone, of course, but the person in the traffic division did tell me where I was likely to find the truck. Even gave me the phone number for the impound lot." Gaby told the trooper about the other calls she had made.

"I'm surprised the medical examiner's office didn't at least let you know that, under the circumstances, Jorgenson's body would wind up at the morgue at Bellevue Hospital in Manhattan. But it's true, you wouldn't have gotten much farther than that without showing up in person."

"Any suggestions on where I should start in New York?" Gaby asked.

"Let me make a few phone calls and get back to you. You going back to the office?"

"I work from home, but I was planning to spend a bit of time at Jorgenson's house up in the Estates this afternoon. I'll be back home after dusk." Gaby gave him her phone number. "Or you could just leave a message. I really appreciate whatever advice you could give me on how to proceed."

"Will do. And hey, while you're up in the Estates, stay alert. We've had a few break-ins reported in that area along with reports of GPS and stereo systems stolen from cars. Probably just kids from Appleton or Prescott home on spring break from college. But be careful."

"Thanks. Maybe I'll bring Kat—my dog—along with me, just for the company and as an early warning system," Gaby replied with a smile.

"Not a bad idea. Have a good day," said the trooper, turning back to his paperwork.

*Wow! Maybe Nell was right. Maybe he will be able to open some doors for me,* Gaby thought, heading back to her car.

Gaby decided to stop at Mike's Place for a sandwich and something to drink, which she planned to take up to Lakeview Terrace to continue her exploration of the house and decide how to handle its contents. As she approached the deli counter, Emma emerged, grabbing Gaby's arm to guide her to one of the tables.

"Have you heard the latest?" she asked Gaby.

"Probably not," replied Gaby with a smile. "I've been out of circulation for a few days."

"It's about Mildred Pearson."

"What's going on?"

"She's been arrested! Seems all those rumors about her misman-agement of the town's special funds had more than a grain of truth. I heard she confessed to embezzling close to half a million dollars!"

"You've got to be kidding!"

At fifty-two, Mildred Pearson had held the position of town clerk since she was first elected some twenty years ago, running for the position at the urging of her uncle, who served as mayor of the town until he died several years back. Never married, Mildred lived with her parents, who operated one of Woodson Falls' dairy farms. When they died, she sold the farmstead property and bought a small, modest cottage just off Main Street.

"It's true! It all started when Mildred found herself short of cash to pay a hefty credit card bill. You know she managed the dog fund, right?"

"Uh-huh."

"Well, there was all that money accumulated from dog license fees and only a small amount paid out for license tags, sometimes a little more for repairs to the animal shelter in Appleton. All that money just sitting there. So, Mildred figured she could take a check from the back of the checkbook, make it out to 'cash,' and send it to a bank she uses over in New York state," Emma continued.

"Oh, my goodness!"

"She planned to cover the debit later. Apparently, the town auditor rarely even looks at the checking statements related to the dog fund. It was a lot of money to Mildred, but a drop in the bucket as far as the town's finances went."

"But still," said Gaby. "It's theft!"

"Exactly. Mildred's scheme worked. A bit of doctoring of the checking statement related to the dog fund and no one was the wiser. If questions arose, she planned to say she used the check to maintain the petty cash fund that took in copying fees, reimbursing the dog fund later with accumulated petty cash. Reasonable enough. But no one asked."

"I know Mildred was town clerk for a long time. I guess people trusted her," said Gaby.

"Right! And the dog fund was only one of several Mildred controlled. So, when she got behind on her bills, she took to 'borrowing' the money she needed from one or another of these funds. And when no one seemed to notice, or care, she didn't worry about restoring the funds right away. After all, she could always take funds from one account to cover another, juggling them so no one was the wiser."

"You've got to be kidding," Gaby said again. "Dowdy Mildred Pearson?"

"Yes, and there's more," Emma continued. "Apparently she conspired with one of the real estate developers to defraud the state and the town of taxes due when building lots were sold."

"Do you know which developer?"

"It's Norman Lutz, the one who developed Woodson Lake Estates. Do you know who he is?"

"I've come across the name. Jorgenson sued him over a drainage issue."

"People started to get suspicious when Mildred began to dress in more expensive clothes, develop a more refined taste in food and drink," Emma went on. "She even traded in her trusty Chevy sedan for a zippy, red Miata! She was spending more and more money, but keeping up with bills through more and more frequent 'borrowing' from the various accounts she maintained."

Lutz lived as large as his sizeable belly. The big-time real estate developer from New York was known for cutting corners and negotiating shady deals. He wined and dined Mildred, making her feel like a princess, not at all in line with her frumpy self-image.

"How was she caught?" Gaby asked.

"Lutz is developing a pretty big tract of land south of Woodson Lake Estates on the Appleton border, much the same way he developed Woodson Lake Estates. Apparently, he sought Mildred's help to reduce his costs when he sold the lots."

"How could she do that?"

"She arranged to file conveyance tax forms that underreported the actual sale prices of the properties. She was more than happy to accommodate Lutz in exchange for his continuing affection."

"That's serious stuff," Gaby exclaimed when Emma had finished telling her all the details. "Did she negotiate a plea deal in exchange for her confession?"

"Apparently. The recommendation the district attorney's office will be making is two years in jail, suspended, five hundred hours of community service, and full restitution of the funds she stole from the town. But only if she reveals the name of the developer."

"And she hasn't done that?"

"Not yet. Standing by her man, I guess, though I doubt he'd do the same for her."

"But doesn't everyone know it's Lutz?" Gaby asked.

"I'm sure they do," Emma answered, "but they can't go after Lutz unless she confirms their arrangement."

"Who would have thought," Gaby mused. "Here in quiet little Woodson Falls."

## Chapter 15

GABY PAID FOR HER TUNA SANDWICH AND DIET PEPSI AND LEFT Mike's Place still pondering Mildred Pearson's situation. What might have prompted such clearly illegal behavior in someone as strait-laced as the former town clerk? Gaby's watch told her that returning home to pick up Kat would leave her too little time to fully investigate the rest of Jorgenson's house before dark, and she wanted to finish as much as possible today. Despite the trooper's warning, she headed straight to Lakeview Terrace alone, planning to leave before dusk set in.

Lakeview Terrace looked barren as she made her way toward Jorgenson's house—no cars on the road, the houses shuttered. None of the summer residents seemed to have arrived and the few full-time residents, including Angela Markham, were either locked behind closed doors or out and about, enjoying this first day of spring-like weather. It seemed odd to Gaby that no one was puttering around the lawn, picking up downed branches, inspecting shrubs for winter damage, looking for signs of the first bulbs—crocus, snowdrops—pushing through the winter soil.

The house smelled musty when Gaby entered, the sunlight filtering into the large main room at the upper level of the house. Things appeared exactly as she had left them less than a week ago, with no evidence of vandalism, at least on this level. She had obtained vacant house insurance on the building, but didn't want the contents disturbed by pranksters invading the space, especially before she had the chance to document what was there and secure any valuables.

Putting down her briefcase and purse on a nearby chair, Gaby went across the breezeway to check out the garage. The old Jeep was sitting there as she remembered it, surrounded by empty water bottles. On a workbench next to the vehicle was an instruction manual on how to restore a 1941 Willy's MB Jeep. An array of what looked like automobile components suggested that Jorgenson might have been restoring the vehicle. It seemed he had his fingers in lots of pies.

*Or maybe he was just desperate to make money beyond the sale of those birdhouses at Frank's store.* She remembered the birdhouses he had been building. *Although with all that cash sitting in the bank... makes you wonder.*

Finding nothing more of interest in the garage, Gaby locked up and went back to the house. Beginning in the kitchen area, she opened cabinets and drawers, noting the contents: a set of dishes with a floral design, coffee mugs, glasses, cutlery, battered pots and pans, utensils, dish towels, paper towels—nothing out of the ordinary. The store of food was equally unremarkable: dry cereal, instant coffee, sugar, a dozen or more boxed juices with straws, cans of soup, chili, spaghetti, graham crackers, and a pile of snack packs of animal crackers.

*Well, Dad hoards Fig Newtons and Mom has the corner on the Snickers market. To each his own, I guess.*

At about six weeks after Jorgenson's death, Gaby expected the pungent odor that arose when she opened the refrigerator, but it still caused her to take a step back. Nothing special there either: sour milk, moldy bread, packaged cold cuts with a greenish tint, butter, dried-up oranges that were fuzzy with age, withered apples, moldy cheese, cans of beer. Several frozen meals were stacked in the freezer, not unusual for a man living alone.

*I'll deal with getting rid of all of this later, maybe order a dumpster. And I'll need a plan for getting all those water bottles to recycling.*

Jorgenson didn't seem to have regular garbage pickup, perhaps taking his trash with him when he went to New York. He could have easily taken the plastic bottles to the recycling center in Prescott, but once they piled up, maybe it seemed too much to bother with.

She wandered over to the workbench positioned in front of the picture windows to the left of the kitchen. She picked up one of the unfinished birdhouses, picturing Jorgenson bent over the table, laboring on one of these avian dwellings.

Putting the birdhouse down, she picked up one of the child-like figures, a girl. There was something familiar about her. *I think it's the dress.*

Gaby went over to her purse and pulled out the box of photos she had brought to show Nell. Shuffling through them, she came to the one Nell had identified as having been taken at Bensonhurst Park. The one showing the metal fish arrayed along a fence with the little girl to the right of the fish with the strange name. The pattern on the girl's dress looked identical to the pattern of the dress on the wooden figure she held in her hand.

*Strange. I wonder what that's about? Did Jorgenson search for fabric similar to this little girl's dress? But why?*

Gaby put figure down and the photos back in her purse, then headed toward the hallway, approaching the door leading to the lower level of the house, her briefcase slung over her shoulder. According to Rusty, this level, which was between the upper floor living area and the basement, held "all kinds of stuff." Whether any of it had value remained to be seen.

*Here goes.*

She hoped the lower level offered windows like those on this upper level and that they would let in the sun. Otherwise, she'd have to rely on any electric lighting that might be available. She carried a flashlight in her briefcase, but doubted it would be adequate to the task of identifying assets and their possible value.

Pausing at the door, she hesitated going downstairs, uncertain of what she might find there.

*Silly girl. You stopped looking for monsters under the bed long ago.* Yet the same anxiety seemed to be deterring her now, the nervousness she was feeling similar to how she felt when facing those old childhood fears.

Officer Thomas might have been right. She probably should have brought along Kat or another person. The only other time she had been in the house, Rusty had been there as well. She hadn't realized how alone and vulnerable she would feel exploring the house alone and wished for Kat's comforting presence.

"Here goes," she said out loud, warning off any demons—or intruders—that might be lurking below.

A light switch on the wall close to the door turned on the bare bulb that lit the stairwell. The landing led directly to a large room, while the stairs continued down to the basement, which Gaby had no intention of exploring today.

Pieces of furniture were scattered about the second-level room that was dominated by a large fireplace along the far wall. Windows stretched along the lakeside of the house, yet the trees surrounding the building partially blocked the sunlight from coming into the dimly lit room. There were no overhead lighting fixtures, but floor lamps had been placed along the walls. Gaby went around the room, turning them on. Together with the windows, the lamps provided plenty of light to guide her exploration.

Aside from furniture forming a sitting area around the fireplace, there seemed to be no rhyme or reason for the collection of mostly antique furniture and equally antique medical equipment that occupied the rest of the space.

Gaby was no expert on antique furniture, but she recognized an intricately carved hat tree, its mirror filmed over with dust, as well as a Victorian-style rolltop desk. Other large wooden pieces seemed to be collected in one area, and she was certain there was value there.

*I'll have to get an antiques appraiser in to give me a sense of the prices some of these items might fetch.*

Grouped haphazardly in another area were an old-fashioned dental chair, a metal cabinet that probably had housed dental supplies, and a collection of wooden wheelchairs that surrounded the other pieces, including several medical office cabinets with glass doors, and an iron lung.

*I wonder how he got that thing down here.*

The odd assortment seemed to confirm Jorgenson's apparent interest in medicine, suggested by the medical supply catalogues in his accumulated mail.

Further exploration revealed a large box in one corner of the room containing miniature wooden wishing wells. Gaby recalled a clipping she had seen in Jorgenson's files upstairs touting similar wishing wells as a good moneymaker when decorated with artificial flowers.

*But there must be hundreds of them here.* None were decorated.

Gaby sat down on the sofa near the fireplace and pulled out a legal pad. She began to catalogue the room's contents. An internet search probably would give her a sense of the value of some of the pieces for the inventory to be submitted to the probate court. She decided to take pictures of the pieces that seemed valuable. She had left her cell phone in her purse upstairs. Heading toward the stairs to retrieve her purse, she was startled by a loud noise coming from above. She stood stock-still, her heart pounding in her ears.

*What was that? Oh, no! I didn't lock the front door after I came in!*

As she crept up the stairs, she heard the shouts of garbage men down the road and the grinding sound of the truck. *Routine pickup, at least I hope that's what it is.*

She breathed a sigh of relief and grabbed her purse, locking the front door before heading back down to the second level. She had carried a spray canister of mace in her purse ever since the attack that killed Joe, but a lot of good that would do her if her purse was upstairs while she was downstairs.

*How could I be so careless?*

Her eye had been drawn to the fireplace when she first stepped into this lower level of the house. Now as she rounded the staircase and came back into the room, she noticed a walled-off area opposite the fireplace and the collection of furniture, equipment and boxes.

*I wonder what's behind this?* she thought as she approached the wall.

*Utilities? No. Rusty said they were in the basement. Bedroom? Office?*

She spotted a door at the far end of the wall and tried the door-knob. It was locked. She hunted around nearby for a key, opening drawers and feeling along the backs of furniture in case the key was hanging nearby but out of sight. She hadn't come across any keys in her search of the upstairs level and wondered whether Jorgenson kept the key to this door with him along with the keys to the house. If that were the case, then the key to this room might be with his personal effects, which she hoped to retrieve if and when she was able to locate his body.

*Either that or I'll have to call on Rusty again to have him break in this door.*

Taking her phone from her purse, Gaby set about photographing several of the antique pieces as well as the most intriguing medical items as she nibbled on her sandwich and sipped her soda. It was near-ing dusk when she finally was finished, satisfied that she had captured images of the more important and, likely, most valuable pieces.

She turned off the floor lamps and headed back up the stairs, clos-ing the door behind her and making her way into the main room. After locking the front door and testing to be sure it was secure, she was climbing up the driveway and walking toward the loaner car she was driving when she spotted a white van with New York plates parked in front of a house down the road from her car.

Gaby started toward the van to check for possible damage from the hit-and-run that had sent her own car to the shop. She was half-way there when a tall man emerged from the house, heading toward the van. Rising panic stopped her. She wasn't close enough to read the van's tag number and wasn't ready for a confrontation with the man who resembled the person she had spotted at the Sunshine Café, clearly the owner of the vehicle that just might have been the one that ran her off the road that same night.

*Oh, boy! I wish I had listened to Officer Thomas and brought Kat with me*, she thought, running back toward her car.

# Chapter 16

THE TALL MAN ROUNDED THE VAN, HEADING TOWARD GABY. A long knife glinted in his hand as he strode in her direction. Gaby picked up her pace, which was quickly matched by her pursuer. She made it to the car, jumped in and locked the doors just as he shook the door handle, menacing her with the knife. He shouted at her, but she was unable to distinguish what he was saying.

She fumbled to get the key in the ignition, finally making contact and taking off down Lakeview Terrace. So did her pursuer—his van racing behind her, threatening to push her off the road. She sped up but couldn't elude him. Feeling the screech as bumper hit bumper, she tried to swerve away, but the van was relentless. She skidded on a turn and lost control of the car, careening over the edge of the road, tumbling down a steep ravine.

She stirred as Kat nudged her awake. The phone jangled loudly. In a sweat, shaking off the remnants of the nightmare, she murmured, "Gaby Quinn."

"Hi there, Ms. Quinn. You okay? Dave calling again, from Teddy's Garage?"

"Good morning, Dave." Gaby ran her fingers through her hair, then through Kat's fur, silently thanking the dog for waking her from the nightmare.

"Just wanted you to know your Subaru is ready. You can bring the loaner down this morning and pick her up. Or someone can bring your car to you, but that won't be until later this afternoon."

"I won't be able to drive to Prescott this morning," responded Gaby, still unsettled by the dream and continuing to run her hand over Kat's soft coat. "I'd appreciate someone bringing my car to me. I gave you my credit card to cover the deductible when I was down there."

"Yup. I have that noted. You'll want to look over the car when you get it. Make sure everything is okay. Just let us know if we've missed anything."

"Will do, and thanks for the call."

Gaby hung up the phone and grabbed her running gear. Maybe a long run with Kat would sweep away the remaining wisps of her dream.

The phone was ringing when she returned home after a five-mile run. The crisp, fresh morning air had cleared her head and she felt ready to face the day.

"Law offices, Gabriella Quinn speaking," she answered.

"Gaby. Good morning. Winston Pinkham here. I was wondering if I might meet with you in the next few days. I'd like to make some changes to my will," a gravelly voice responded.

"Sure, Mr. Pinkham. Would tomorrow work for you? I could be at your house by ten, unless you'd prefer the afternoon."

"Hmm… I'm expecting my accountant at nine and I'm not certain how long that will take. How about we say two, or three?"

"Either would work for me. Why not make it for two and if you find yourself pressed for time just let me know and we'll bump it to three. Would that be okay?"

"That would be fine, Gaby. I really appreciate your coming to the house, you know. Saves me a trek into town."

"No problem, Mr. Pinkham. I'm happy to come to you. I'll see you tomorrow afternoon, and we can discuss the changes you want to make to your will."

"Until tomorrow then. Bye now, Gaby."

"Goodbye, and have a good day. It's beautiful out. Maybe you can take a walk in your garden. See if anything is popping up," she said before hanging up, knowing Pinkham was unlikely to take her advice.

With a subtle sense of humor under a gruff exterior, Pinkham had once been outgoing and involved in the community, especially in organizations seeking to preserve open space in an effort to prevent Woodson Falls from becoming just one more bedroom community. That changed when he sold the family homestead to two New Yorkers, moved to a cottage that was said to be the first house ever built in Woodson Falls, and became increasingly reclusive, rarely venturing outdoors to enjoy the cottage's wooded setting.

Gaby had been surprised when Pinkham first called to ask her to draw up his will. When she met with him, he told her that the attorney who had drafted his charitable remainder trust kept putting off Pinkham's requests to meet regarding his will. He liked the fact that Gaby was local and said he wanted to help get her practice off the ground. She was even more surprised when he handed her a check for three times the amount she had requested.

"You're charging too little," he'd growled. "People will never value your services if you don't put a steep enough price on them."

Gaby pulled Pinkham's bulky file from her desk. Never married, Pinkham was an only child with just two cousins still living. Even so, his will divided his estate among close to twenty beneficiaries, each receiving a percentage of the estate assets, a percentage that varied with his mood and whether one or another of them had sent a birthday or Christmas card. This would be the fourth revision of the will, which only got more complex over time. It was unlikely to be the last.

"I wonder what new wrinkle he'll add this time," she mumbled to herself, setting aside the file to review prior to their meeting tomorrow afternoon.

Gaby made a cup of tea and settled in to work on the Connecticut probate court's Form PC-440 on which she would be reporting the inventory of assets for the Jorgenson estate. She had already gathered the required information except for the antique furniture she'd discovered on the house's lower level.

*Was that just yesterday?*

She surfed the internet to determine an approximate value of the larger pieces, entering a lump sum for the various items of tangible personal property found in the house other than the vehicles. She could always revise the inventory later if she came across any other valuable property.

Setting aside the completed form, she planned the trip she would need to take to New York City, beginning with a list detailing what she wanted to accomplish.

First on her list was to locate Jorgenson's body and arrange for its transportation to Connecticut. She'd need to contact Jorgenson's Uncle Lucas again to see if he had any preferences regarding funeral home and burial site. She recalled him saying that Jorgenson would want to be buried near his mother, but Gaby had neglected to ask Lucas where that was. Once she had that information, she'd contact the funeral home to make final arrangements. All of this would need to be in place before she traveled to New York.

She wondered whether it would have been the medical examiner's office or the police who secured Jorgenson's personal possessions. She hoped to locate his wallet, any keys—especially to the lower-level room—and anything else that might indicate what Jorgenson was doing in New York, a detail that nagged at her. Perhaps someone in the medical examiner's office would tell her which police precinct had been involved in finding his body so she could ask the police for details surrounding its discovery.

While the medical examiner's office was her most important stop, she did want to talk with the police who had found Jorgenson. Where had he been when his body had been discovered, and who had discovered it? Was there any indication of foul play? What were their general impressions of the situation? Something niggled at the back of her mind that suggested there were more pieces to the puzzle of Jorgenson than she had uncovered so far. Nell had taught her not to ignore her intuition even as she pursued a case in a disciplined manner. Right now, her intuition seemed to be asking her to look deeper, that there was more here than met the eye.

Gaby's last stop would be the impound lot. She wanted to search the truck Jorgenson had taken to the city for anything that might be left in the vehicle, although the police would probably have secured these items. She planned to pay the impound fee and ask that the vehicle be auctioned, with any proceeds sent to Gaby as the administrator of the estate. That meant calling Manhattan Impound again to update the accumulating fees to release the vehicle so she could arrive prepared with a certified check for the amount.

Although it was early, Gaby still hadn't heard from Officer Thomas and assumed she'd be making this foray into New York with limited information to guide her. The trooper might be able to open a door or two or point her to the right precinct, but that was the most she could expect.

She pulled up a map of lower Manhattan on the internet and located the places she would be visiting.

Bellevue Hospital, which housed the M.E.'s office, was on First Avenue and Twenty-Seventh Street, a fairly direct bus ride from Grand Central since she planned to take the train into the city rather than drive and have to deal with parking the car somewhere. The Ninth Police Precinct was on East Fifth Street, a reasonable distance to walk from Bellevue. If she needed to go to the Sixth Precinct, located on West Tenth Street, she could reach there on foot as well.

The doorbell interrupted her planning.

"Ms. Quinn?" the young man asked when she opened the door. "I'm Pete, from Teddy's Garage. I brought back your car a bit earlier than we anticipated. Hope that's okay."

"Great," she answered. "Let me get you the keys to the loaner."

She handed the keys to the young man and stepped out of the house to look her car over. The fender and bumper had been replaced. With the doors repaired, the damage was invisible actually. Beyond that, she wasn't sure what had been done and sent a questioning glance at Pete.

"We realigned the tires and made sure the steering and brakes were okay. She drove real nice on the way up here, but if you run into any problems, just give us a call."

"Well, thank you. I'm sure everything is fine."

Stepping back into the house, Gaby resumed work on her New York itinerary.

She didn't think it would be feasible to walk to Pier 76, where the Manhattan Impound was located, especially given the walking she planned to do earlier in the visit. Located off the West Side Highway at Thirty-Fourth Street, getting to the lot from lower Manhattan would require a taxi or Uber ride. From there, though, she could hop a bus back to the train station.

If the weather holds—it would take a lot of jockeying around if it was raining. Or she could just defer the visit to a clear day. It's not like she had any appointments to keep.

Gazing out the window as the day gradually dissolved into dusk, Gaby drifted back to those early days with Joe in New York. They had walked everywhere, absorbing all the sights and sounds of the city, exploring pocket parks, sampling the many niche restaurants tucked away along the streets, poking into antique stores in search of quirky odds and ends that served as conversation pieces in their apartment, meeting after work for a glass of wine before heading home.

"C'mon, Gab. We're celebrating," he'd said, pulling her into their favorite bar. "Champagne for my lady and me." He'd winked at Gaby as he gave the order to the bartender.

"What's the occasion, Joe?" She'd grinned at his boyish excitement.

"They loved it, Gaby! Especially the social media tie-in we were able to develop. Lots of ad firms are having trouble with that piece, and we nailed it."

She smiled at the memory of Joe's enthusiastic description of the creative advertising campaign the team he headed up had just completed for a new client.

"That's great! I know you've been working hard on this one."

They had ended up going out to dinner, walking home under a moonlit night.

Gaby turned back to her desk to make a "to do" list for tomorrow, but found her hands trembling so much she was unable to hold her pen to paper. She felt her heart rate accelerate along with her breathing, recognizing the signs of what her therapist had labeled post-traumatic stress disorder.

She had worked hard to bury those feelings of despair and vulnerability deep inside so she could function, but they emerged every now and again, like now, so strongly that it was hard to regain control before they developed into a full-fledged panic attack. Running usually helped to ease those feelings, but it was too dark to take a run now.

Gaby got up from her desk and began pacing. Sensing her distress, the dog came to her and leaned against her leg. "Oh, Kat. What a joy you are! Come snuggle with me a bit until I can find a way to de-stress."

*What now?* she thought as she lay against the dog, whose warmth helped to stop her trembling. *Make cookies? Watch TV?*

Gaby settled on taking a shower in an effort to scrub away her tension, allowing her tears to flow with the hot water as it circled down the drain.

## Chapter 17

GABY'S HEART RATE HAD FINALLY SLOWED HALF AN HOUR LATER. Dressed in the flannel pajama pants and sweatshirt she favored on cool nights like this, she poured a glass of white wine, put on some soft jazz, and lit the fire she had laid in the stone fireplace in the den. She was glad she hadn't converted the fireplace to propane when she remodeled the cottage. She loved the snap and crackle of the burning wood as well as its smoky aroma.

Kat snuggled up against her on the love seat, the dog's warmth helping to offset the inner chill Gaby still felt, a remnant of her panic. The pale beige paint she had chosen for the den walls highlighted the dark walnut of the built-in bookcases surrounding the fireplace, the warm colors complemented by the rusts and greens of the furniture. Plump velveteen pillows and patchwork lap quilts were an invitation to relax, listen to music, read a book, or just stare into the fire.

Her thoughts drifted back to the good memories of Joe and their life in New York. They had set up a game table in their apartment, on which stretched a thousand-piece jigsaw puzzle they worked on intermittently. She smiled remembering their totally different styles of puzzling. She diligently searched out all the border pieces, placing them in a pile before trying to fit them together. Joe grabbed a handful of pieces and began putting them together based on color or the corner of some object depicted on the puzzle box. He positioned the several pieces he'd managed to lock together in the appropriate section of the puzzle, while she avoided looking at the picture on the box, trusting it would emerge as the puzzle was completed. So different in their approaches to both work and play—a study in contrasts that somehow worked as a successful merger.

They had both gone to Columbia but didn't date then, just ended up in a group that met for lunch in the cafeteria or went out together on the weekend. He graduated two years ahead of her and entered the business world while she continued her studies at Columbia. They met again several years later at the wedding of mutual friends and began to date. They made a handsome couple, both dark-haired—he a lean six-foot-four, just the right height for her to snuggle under his arm.

After Joe was killed, she found notes he had scribbled on scraps of paper. They were everywhere, ideas for one or another ad campaign, some with diagrams outlining a strategy that might or might not work, others with sketches of possible logos or packaging ideas. He usually carried a small notepad to capture the creative bursts that came to him at odd times. If the notepad wasn't available, he'd make do with a napkin, a corner torn off the newspaper or magazine he was reading, the back of his hand, his sleeve. He'd once said that writing down an idea helped him to recall it later, even if he couldn't find the actual written words. Other times, he'd stumble across an old note that took him in a new creative direction.

The night Joe had won the new account and they'd celebrated, first with champagne, then with dinner, they were so absorbed in each other as they walked home that they didn't even notice the man with the knife heading toward them. Before they had realized anything, he had slashed Gaby's face and stabbed Joe in the chest. That's when she finally caught a glimpse of the tall attacker as he ran toward a white van, jumped into the driver's seat, and pulled away from the curb. If they had caught the man who knifed them or even identified a possible motive for the attack, she might not be having these irrational reactions so many years later to every tall stranger she saw or any white van she spotted sporting New York plates.

A detective had visited her in the hospital where she was recuperating after surgery. They'd had to stitch up the five-inch slash that just missed her eye, ending before reaching her mouth. Then there was the process of healing her ankle, broken when Joe collapsed on top of her after he was knifed. Although the attack was captured on one of the street corner cameras that proliferated in the city, the license plate was blurred and no one came forward with information. She hadn't been able to provide the police with any possible motive for either of them to be targeted. Who would attack an ad man and a college professor? Nothing had been taken, Joe's wallet still in his pants pocket, her handbag intact, no jewelry pulled from her neck.

"We'll keep the case file open," the detective said, "just in case we can tie this attack to another. But I have to warn you, ma'am, it's doubtful. It most likely was a random act. Too much of that going on these days. Sorry I can't give you a sense of closure."

She hated that word. Closure. As if a door could be gently latched against her grief.

The facial wound was deep, down to the bone. There had been some nerve damage, many stitches, and significant blood loss. The resulting anemia and dizziness, coupled with the shock of the attack and Joe's death, compounded her sense of being in a dark place. Lying in the hospital bed, her body just wanted to give up, and she stopped caring whether she lived or died. In fact, she thought at times it might be better to just die, so she could be reunited with Joe.

During the long recovery that followed the reconstruction of her ankle, Gaby was forced to deal with the reality of Joe's death in a more concrete way, particularly the legal and financial implications of her new widowhood and getting the matter through New York's Surrogate Court system. A colleague from Columbia recommended that Gaby consider consulting Attorney Caryn Ellison, who specialized in such matters. Caryn proved to be an invaluable support to

Gaby, gently guiding her through the complex process of shifting ownership of property owned by both Joe and Gaby to Gaby's sole ownership under New York's laws of intestacy. Neither Joe nor Gaby had even thought about having a will, never considering the need for such forward planning since they were young and hadn't yet started a family.

Once she was on the mend, Gaby rethought her decision to pursue the field of philosophy as her parents had and began tinkering with the idea of switching careers completely. It was working with Caryn that led her to finally settle on the law as offering her the possibility of a career that was both intellectually challenging and exact, as well as providing an opportunity to help others. It had been a mostly satisfying change.

During those law school years, she realized that, unlike her younger classmates, she had no interest in winning at all costs and making a lot of money along the way. Having had a successful academic career, Gaby knew she didn't want to work in a law office tallying eighty billable hours a week in order to be made partner. Together with the inheritance from her grandfather and the hefty life insurance settlement from Joe's company, she could afford to charge modestly for her efforts, hoping to meet the expenses of operating her law practice without having to be concerned about socking away a lot of money.

Moving to Woodson Falls after finishing law school had been good for her, both physically and emotionally. She began taking care of herself, eating wisely, getting exercise, engaging with the community, and reconnecting with those long ago, summertime friends who still lived in Woodson Falls. She filled the empty hours with her law work, choosing the areas of probate and estate planning as those most likely to enable her to work with people at their most vulnerable—when there was a death in terms of administering an estate or when someone was contemplating their own death in terms of estate planning.

She had settled into the rhythm of the small town. Maybe that's why she was dreading this return to New York, fearful that the memories would cascade and immobilize her. Still, she was Jorgenson's personal representative with respect to his estate, which meant she had a duty to fulfill the requirements of that role. And that was a duty she wouldn't shirk.

Nuzzling Kat, she got up from her seat and set some of the Soupe au Pistou she had made earlier on the stove to heat. She fed the dog and let her out, putting together a simple salad to have with the soup while she waited for Kat's scratch on the door. After dinner, such as it was, Gaby returned to her office to attack the backlog of work that had accumulated while she was focused on the Jorgenson estate.

# Chapter 18

IT WAS RAINING WHEN GABY WOKE THE NEXT MORNING, SO SHE deferred her run until later in the afternoon after she returned from seeing Winston Pinkham. She reviewed his file over her second cup of coffee, recalling the most recent changes he had made to his will several months earlier.

Placing the file in her briefcase along with a fresh legal pad, she organized her desk for the work she had planned for later that afternoon and dressed for the visit. She wanted to check with the building and health departments at the town hall to determine the status of Jorgenson's well and septic, then stop for a quick lunch at the Sunshine Café before heading to Pinkham's place off Sunrise Trail in the woods bordering New York state.

It was grey and gloomy as she drove toward town, a steady rain falling, running in rivulets on the sides of the road. She pulled up the hood of her raincoat as she exited the car and jogged the few feet to the town hall entrance from where she had parked, her ankle throbbing as it often did in weather like this.

Waving to Martie Rubin as she passed the town clerk's office, where Martie was busy accepting documents for filing, Gaby made her way to Miriam Henderson's office opposite the tax collector. Miriam was responsible for maintaining the records related to the status of zoning, wetlands, building and health permits on each of Woodson Falls' five or six hundred properties.

"Thanks for dinner the other night, Sally," she called to the tax collector before turning into the land use office. "Let's do it again, soon. My place next time."

"You're on," Sally responded.

"Hi, Miriam," she said, entering the office. "How've you been?"

Miriam looked up from a desk piled high with folders. "Fine, thanks. You here about Pinkham's subdivision? I seem to recall him mentioning that you were helping him with his will, but I thought Bill Harrison was handling the legal work on the subdivision."

"Subdivision?"

"He's carving out six lots on the property abutting his house. I'd heard he'd earmarked that land to give to the Woodson Falls Land Trust, but I guess he had second thoughts."

"Well, I don't do land use law. He was wise to engage Bill. He's tops in his field," she said, smiling and making a mental note to discuss this change in plans with Pinkham when she saw him this afternoon. Perhaps that was why he wanted to see her. "Actually, I'm here about a property in Woodson Lake Estates, number sixteen Lakeview Terrace. I'm wondering about the status of the property with respect to well and septic permits."

Miriam got up from her desk and went over to the long horizontal files lining one wall of the office. A dozen or more maps depicting plot plans stood in the corner. More were piled on top of the files. She pulled out the drawer containing the records for each property in Woodson Falls.

"Here's the file. Owner's a Pieter Jorgenson. Apparently built the structure himself. Difficult land up there."

"You can say that again! Not sure how he even got a cement truck up there, never mind poured the footings."

"Okay. Here we are." Miriam opened the file on the counter separating her workspace from the public. "Deeps and percs were done, so the land has decent enough drainage to support a septic, and Jorgenson pulled permits for both that and a well, but there's no record of the work being done. He needs an engineered septic to deal with the terrain."

"No C.O. issued, I assume," Gaby said, referring to the certificate of occupancy that rendered a structure legally habitable.

"Nope," Miriam replied. "Not without a well and septic. Zoning signed off on the property awhile back, so the structure is in conformity. Building signed off on the electric and heating work as well as the foundation some time ago. Wonder what Jorgenson's waiting for."

"I'm handling his estate, so it'll be a while longer. Ground's still too frozen to begin that kind of work anyway."

"Now I remember. Sally mentioned something in passing about him dying. Too bad. Nice piece of property up there. Great views."

"It *is* pretty. The contrast of the falls against the surrounding hills and forest is unique, and the lake seems to shimmer from that high up. Anyway, thanks for the information. I suspected the well and septic were still outstanding. He's been using bottled water and goodness knows where waste is going."

"A lot of people up in the Estates don't bother with a septic. They use dry wells instead, although that's not allowed in the health code. Want copies of the permits?"

"I'll come back to review the file when I'm ready to offer the property for sale. I still have a few issues to clear up before I can do that," she said, leaving the office. *Like finding his body and getting him buried, for starters.* "Thanks for your help."

Gaby wondered if the assessor had considered the lack of a well and septic in estimating the value of the property, but the door to Osborn's office was closed when she passed it as she left the building. She would have to come back to check on that when she was closer to putting the property on the market. The engineered septic would be expensive and, depending on where it ended up being located, the well might require an expensive pumping system. Not her problem, but the logistics and expenses involved in getting those two systems installed on the steep lot would likely lower the potential sale price of the property.

Peggy Huntington greeted Gaby effusively when she entered the Sunshine Café. "Thanks so much for helping Walter out. He's such a good worker. I'd hate to lose him."

"It really wasn't anything, Peggy. Just helping a friend," Gaby responded. "Any specials on the menu today?"

"I'd recommend the mac and cheese on a day like today. That would warm your insides. I've even topped it with bits of bacon, your favorite."

"Sounds perfect. I'll have that and a cup of herbal tea," Gaby said, sliding onto one of the stools to eat at the counter. While she ate, she leafed through the latest issue of the bar association's monthly magazine, musing on the possibilities presented by Pinkham's subdivision. Like some of her other elderly clients who lacked close relatives or friends who might serve as executor of their wills, Pinkham had asked if Gaby would serve in this role. She had accepted and now wondered how his subdivision plans might complicate administering the will's provisions. There would be no issue if the lots were sold before his death, but if they remained on the market after he died, the estate could be tied up for months.

Entering Winston Pinkham's cottage, Gaby took off her raincoat, hanging it on a hook in the small foyer.

"It's Gaby Quinn, Mr. Pinkham," Gaby called, slipping off her shoes to avoid tracking rain and mud on the oriental rugs that were scattered about the wide-plank oak floor of his living room. The room was filled with Colonial-style furniture, the walls papered in a dusty rose motif that had faded with sunlight and time.

"Ah, come in, come in," he answered.

As she entered the living room, Gaby found Pinkham sitting in his usual spot, a well-worn wingback chair, smoking a cigarette. The oxygen condenser at his side continued to chug away, the nasal cannula and tubing running to the condenser dangling from his neck.

"Mr. Pinkham!" Gaby exclaimed. "Trying to blow up the place?"

"Hello there, Gaby. I'm too old to break a lifelong habit, even with this... What do they call it? Emphysema. Besides, I'm about ready to die anyway," he said, stubbing out the cigarette and gesturing to Gaby to take a seat beside him.

Several years ago, Pinkham had begun announcing his impending death to anyone within earshot, but had yet to make good on his prediction. True, he had advanced lung disease as well as early prostate cancer, but at eighty-nine he still managed his own affairs, with a neighbor doing the shopping and bringing an occasional hot meal.

"How did your meeting with your accountant go this morning?"

"It went well, I suppose. Barney says I have enough money to make it to a hundred and beyond. But I'm worried."

"Worried?"

"I'm not sure I have enough money to go to one of those 'waiting-to-die' places."

"You mean a hospice?"

"Is that what they call it? I've been looking at brochures from a number of those places, but the costs are enormous."

"Did you know that you can get the same care in your home if you need it? The Prescott Visiting Nurse Service just started a home hospice program. All the costs are covered by Medicare, and you can stay in your own house."

"Really? Ah, well... In any event, I've decided to subdivide the land I own south of this property and sell off the lots, just to be sure there's enough. I've asked Bill Harrison to help me with the subdivision. It's only six lots, but if I'm able to sell them, the profit may be just enough to carry me through. That's what I wanted to talk with you about, Gaby."

"Okay. The article in your will that gifts that property to the land trust will have to be changed, of course. What did you have in mind?"

"Here's what I'm thinking," Pinkham replied.

## Chapter 19

THE SUN WAS PEEKING OUT OF THE CLOUDS AS GABY HEADED home from seeing Winston Pinkham. She quickly changed into her running clothes and called Kat to take their postponed run while there was still a break in the weather. Running along Pine Hill Road to its intersection with Route 41 rather than on the soggy ground through the woods, Gaby thought about the latest changes Pinkham wanted to make to his will.

He planned to offer two friends a steep discount on the price of specific lots in exchange for their help with the subdivision, and he wanted that offer reflected in his will. Both individuals had expressed an interest in the properties, but there was no guarantee they would be able to pay the remaining cost. It seemed an odd decision for someone concerned about running out of funds, but it was his decision to make and one unlikely to affect the administration of Pinkham's will after he died.

It was still chilly and damp as Gaby turned to head for home, the steely grey clouds promising another burst of rain, which began to fall just as she and Kat reached Beaver Trail and her cottage. Feeling refreshed from her run, Gaby filled Kat's water bowl and brewed a cup of tea, taking it to her office.

First on today's "to do" list was a call to Jorgenson's Uncle Lucas to determine where Jorgenson's mother was buried and identify the funeral home that had made the arrangements. Transportation of a decedent's remains over state lines had to be done between funeral homes. She'd gotten an estimate of the potential costs of transferring Jorgenson's body from New York to Connecticut. It was a surprisingly large amount, but she had sufficient money in the estate account into which she had moved all the funds from Jorgenson's bank accounts.

Lucas' answering machine picked up on the fourth ring.

"Good afternoon, Mr. Jorgenson. This is Gabriella Quinn, the attorney handling your nephew's estate. I was wondering if you could give me a call with the name of the funeral home that handled your sister Sofia's funeral and the cemetery where she is buried. I plan to go into New York later this week and hope to begin the process of bringing Pieter's remains home to Connecticut." She repeated her name and gave her phone number, as well as her request that Lucas call her back when he was able.

She suspected that Jorgenson had already been buried on New York's Hart Island, in which case she'd have to get a court order to exhume the body for burial elsewhere if that's what his family wanted. There was a slim chance his body had been offered to one of the local medical schools, but that would only happen if an autopsy hadn't been required. The only way she would get an answer to this basic question was to present the documents naming her as the administrator of Jorgenson's estate to the officials at the morgue, which was one reason she had to travel to New York.

Gaby was in the middle of drafting the new clause for Pinkham's will when the phone rang.

"Law offices. Gabriella Quinn speaking," she said, her mind still on the wording she planned to incorporate in Pinkham's will.

"Hi, Ms. Quinn. Matt Thomas calling."

"Officer Thomas! How can I help you?"

"I'm hoping I can help you," he responded. "I checked around and found someone at the Ninth Precinct who might be able to answer some of your questions about Pieter Jorgenson, the case you spoke to me about."

"Really? Wow! That's fantastic," Gaby exclaimed, a bit surprised but pleased that the resident trooper had followed through with his offer to make some inquiries after their brief conversation.

"The officer I spoke with at the Ninth was one of the detectives involved with the case. His name is Bradford Wilkinson, and he said he'd be glad to talk with you, provided there's nothing big going on. I'd be happy to set up a meeting for you. When were you planning to go into New York?"

"I was hoping to get there sometime this week. I haven't planned anything definite yet."

"I'm off in a few days. Would you like some company? I could drive you in, and we could figure out the best way to proceed after you talk with Detective Wilkinson."

"You'd do that?" Gaby exclaimed, wondering why Thomas would make such an offer, but jumping at the possibility of not making the trip on her own.

"Sure. After all, Jorgenson was a Woodson Falls resident. I'm kinda curious about just what happened to him. Plus, I can probably smooth the way for you at the Ninth."

"It would be great to have the company and at least a place to start. Thanks so much, both for following up and for offering to go along with me."

"It would be my pleasure, Ms. Quinn. And, can I ask you, please? Just call me Matt."

"Sure. It's Gaby. Let me know when you're off and we'll take it from there."

"Great. I'll give you a call, probably tomorrow. Any time better for you?"

"No. I was planning to work in the office tomorrow."

"Bye, Gaby."

"Thanks again, Officer... I mean, Matt. Goodbye."

Hanging up, Gaby was delighted as well as a bit flustered with Thomas' offer. She couldn't imagine why he would take the time to do this. Still, she was happy not to be going into the city alone. Having at least one door opened for her was a bonus she never anticipated. That alone would make the trip easier.

She and Matt had settled on Tuesday morning of the following week for the trip to New York. The night before, Gaby packed her briefcase in preparation for the visit. Officer Thomas—she'd have to get used to calling him Matt, although that still felt uncomfortable—would be picking her up at 8:30, plenty of time to arrive at the Ninth Precinct for the meeting with Detective Wilkinson scheduled for 10:30. She had several copies of the probate court documents appointing her as the administrator of Jorgenson's estate, certified copies of his death certificate, and the title to the truck being held at the Manhattan Impound.

She had heard from Lucas, who told her Sofia was buried at Evergreen Cemetery in Prescott. The Wallace Funeral Home, also in Prescott, had made the arrangements. She spoke with someone there and had the contact information necessary to arrange for the transportation of Jorgenson's remains from New York. She had called Manhattan Impound for an update on fees to be paid to release Jorgenson's truck and had a certified check for that amount. She added a fresh legal pad to the briefcase and snapped it shut.

"Should be an interesting day," she murmured to herself. She just hoped that being with someone would quiet her nerves. She didn't want to have to explain her jitters to Officer Thomas.

The clouds that had shrouded the skies for the past few days had cleared overnight. The sun shone brightly, and it had warmed considerably by the time Gaby finished her morning run with Kat and dressed for the trip to New York. The dog bounded to the door when the doorbell rang, wagging her tail.

"Some guard dog you are," Gaby said, opening the door. "Come on in, Matt. I just need to grab my coat."

"What a gorgeous dog!" Matt exclaimed, bending to first let Kat sniff his hand and then giving her a rub, which the dog leaned into as if the trooper was a long-lost friend.

"You know dogs, I see," Gaby commented, gathering her briefcase and purse.

"Yeah, we always had one when I was growing up. It's one of the things I missed when I moved to the city. Ready?"

Gaby locked her door, and they headed down the path to Matt's car, an older-model Volkswagen station wagon.

"How's the wagon in the snow and ice?" she asked.

"Not so great. This model doesn't have four-wheel drive, and it isn't great on gas either. I just haven't had the chance to trade it in for something better. I'm mostly in the cruiser anyway."

They made small talk as Matt headed out toward New York's Route 22 and the highway. Traffic was light.

"So… If you don't mind me asking, what do you hope to accomplish in New York?" Matt asked, glancing at Gaby, who was staring out the window, watching the scenery rush past.

"Mostly locate Jorgenson's body and arrange for it to be transferred to Connecticut. And dispose of his truck, but that means a trip to the Manhattan Impound, where I hope to convince them to auction off the truck and send the proceeds to me to add to Jorgenson's estate. I also want to recover his personal effects."

"How do you want to handle this? I mean, after you've had a chance to talk with Wilkinson?"

"I think next go to Bellevue to talk with the medical examiner's office, then the impound. I'm hoping things go smoothly today, and I won't have to make a second trip. Being able to talk with the detective involved with the case will be a big help. Thanks for setting that up and for taking me today."

"Do you go through all this with every estate you handle?"

"Not by a long shot. Usually, I'm working with the executor of the estate, helping with the paperwork, offering suggestions and answering questions. It's ordinarily a smooth process. This one is complicated by the fact that I never met Jorgenson and know virtually nothing about him, but since there was no one available to serve as executor, I'm expected to settle his affairs. One of the first things the probate court asks for is a copy of the funeral bill. I haven't even been able to get that far yet."

"Must be frustrating."

"A bit, but it's also intriguing, uncovering the details of someone's life. In the short time I've been practicing law, I've found each estate has its own surprises. So far, this one's not much different in that respect."

"Surprises?"

"It's just funny what some people manage to accumulate. With one estate I handled, the house was meticulously neat, but the garage was filled with empty cardboard boxes. With this one, it's empty water jugs. You just never know."

# Chapter 20

GABY AND MATT ARRIVED AT THE NINTH PRECINCT WITH TIME to spare. Matt guided the station wagon into an available parking spot across the street from the iconic police station.

"If the building seems familiar, it should be. It's been filmed for a number of television police shows," Matt commented, taking Gaby's elbow and steering her across the street and up the steps.

They entered the building and made their way into the massive muster room, dominated by an imposing desk. Plaques honoring fallen policemen had been mounted with care on the wall behind it.

They confirmed their appointment with Detective Wilkinson and signed in. Wilkinson came out to greet them. At six-foot-seven, he was lean but muscular. His military bearing and shaven head would have been intimidating had it not been for his warm greeting as he escorted them into the open office area.

"Brad," Matt began, "this is Gabriella Quinn, the attorney I spoke with you about. She's handling Pieter Jorgenson's estate and needs some basic information I thought you'd be able to help her with."

"Welcome to the Fighting Ninth, Ms. Quinn. Glad to meet you," Wilkinson said, shaking Gaby's hand. "Hope I can be of assistance."

"Thank you for seeing me. Officer Thomas filled me in on some of the history of the Ninth Precinct during our drive in from Connecticut. You have a lot to be proud of," Gaby replied.

Wilkinson turned to Matt. "Good to see you again, Matt. So sorry to hear about Brenda and your daughter. We were away when it happened. Couldn't make the service. How are you doing?"

"I'm okay. The move out of the city was good for me," Matt responded, his voice subdued.

Gaby looked at Matt, an unasked question in her eyes.

"I pulled the file on Jorgenson to refresh my recollection of the case. It's been a while since my partner and I caught it. Let's go into the conference room, where we'll have a bit of privacy," Wilkinson said, pointing the way with a folder he was holding. They entered a small room that Gaby suspected was one of many interrogation rooms, familiar to anyone who watched police procedurals on television.

Once they were settled, Wilkinson said, "First, let's get past the identification stage. Officer Thomas here indicated that you had been appointed as the executor of Jorgenson's estate?"

"Yes," Gaby responded, opening her briefcase and feeling more prepared than she had been back at the police station in Prescott. "Here's my driver's license and attorney identification, as well as a copy of the official decree from the probate court appointing me as the administrator of the estate, a certified copy of Jorgenson's death certificate, and a fiduciary certificate authorizing me to deal with his property."

"Great. Let me make copies of these for our records." He handed the fiduciary certificate to Matt. "Matt, would you mind going down to the property desk to claim Jorgenson's personal property on Ms. Quinn's behalf? I'll call ahead to let them know you're coming."

"No problem," Matt answered as he headed out the door with Wilkinson, who walked into the inner office to make copies of Gaby's documents, leaving her alone in the conference room.

*Guess this is how people feel after they've been arrested and left to stew,* Gaby thought. *Hard not to feel like you're guilty of something, even knowing you aren't.* She was grateful once again that she hadn't made the trip to New York alone as she struggled to block the anxiety that threatened to take over the longer she sat there.

Wilkinson came back into the room several minutes later and sat down across from Gaby. "Sorry to keep you waiting. Now that we've dispensed with the formalities, how can I help you?"

"Can you tell me anything about how Jorgenson was found? What happened to him, and where his body ended up? I never met the man, and I'm trying to put the pieces of his life together, particularly its end, in addition to getting him buried."

"We responded to a 911 call in the vicinity of Tompkins Square Park. The 911 operator reported that the caller said, quote, 'There's a dude in a truck. Looks dead to me.' The operator told the caller that the police and an ambulance were on the way and asked him to identify himself, but he just went on, 'Hasn't moved for at least half an hour. You better come and check it out.' The operator told the caller to stay near the truck until we got there.

"We arrived at the location ahead of EMS and found a group of kids gathered around a truck with Connecticut plates. A male was in the driver's seat, slumped over the steering wheel. We approached the vehicle and attempted to arouse the individual. My partner felt for a carotid pulse, couldn't find any, and was about to pull the man from the vehicle to begin CPR when EMS arrived at the scene and took over. They packaged him quickly and took him by ambulance to Bellevue. My partner went with the ambulance and learned the individual was pronounced DOA at the hospital. The body was transferred to the morgue. You'd have to check with them on where it went after that."

"Any idea what happened to him?" asked Gaby.

"The kids said the man had been sitting in the truck for a while, watching them play ball. He called one boy over—the one who made the 911 call—and just as the boy approached the car, the man groaned, grabbed his head, then passed out over the steering wheel. The caller said he backed off after the man passed out, then returned a bit later since the truck hadn't moved. That's when he called 911. The medical examiner told my partner it looked like a massive stroke, maybe a ruptured aneurysm."

"What was Jorgenson doing there?"

"That's anybody's guess. The kids said they thought he was waiting for someone. One of the boys said he'd seen him before, at Tompkins and at Hamilton Fish Park, a few blocks away. The boy said he was a 'scary dude, big.'"

"Did you think the boys you talked to were reliable? I guess I'm wondering if Jorgenson was attacked, mugged. Whether something violent happened that the boys weren't talking about."

"Hard to say whether the boys' report was accurate. While the city's cleaned up the park since the riots in the '80s, it still attracts a fair share of the homeless, runaway kids, some addicts and drug dealers. But the medical examiner's preliminary examination didn't reveal any evidence of a beat down or anything like that."

"What happened after the ambulance left?"

"I stayed at the scene, searched the truck, and waited for the tow truck to take it back here for a thorough examination. In the meantime, my partner was at Bellevue to get an identification on the individual and secure any personal effects. We met later at the precinct to work on the report."

"Anything in the truck?"

Wilkinson leafed through the file in front of him. "Let's see here," he said, running his finger down the page he was turned to. "There was a small camera lying on the passenger seat of the truck along with a map of New York City's boroughs. In addition to the registration and insurance card, the glove box contained a tire gauge, small ring-bound notebook, a packet of gum—the usual paraphernalia we all collect. There was a large plastic container behind the passenger's seat with those small cartons of juice with straws like you pick up for children to drink, and snack packs of animal crackers. No evidence of alcohol or even cigarettes. No drugs or drug paraphernalia."

He turned the page. "The truck box in the truck bed was locked, and the key to the ignition was the only key on that keyring. After my partner brought back Jorgenson's wallet and the set of keys he had in his pocket, we were able to open it. The truck box held a fairly large, well-stocked tool kit, like a carpenter would carry. Also, a duffel bag, some large plastic bags, strapping tape. We relocked the truck box, so those items—along with the juice and crackers—are still with the vehicle at Manhattan Impound."

Matt came into the room with a large plastic envelope, which he laid on the table. "The insurance card and registration were secured along with the victim's wallet and keys and should be in there," Wilkinson added, pointing to the plastic evidence envelope lying between Gaby and Wilkinson. "The other items in the glove box and the camera and map were left in the truck. The ignition key went with the truck to Impound."

"Anything else?"

"Not much," Wilkinson said, turning back to the file. "When we went through the wallet, we found a business card for an attorney. He was called and asked to provide the medical examiner with the information needed for the death certificate. Don't remember the attorney's name, but the card should still be with the wallet."

"I can take this?" asked Gaby, placing a hand on the envelope.

"You signed it out, right, Matt?" Wilkinson asked.

"Yup. It's free and clear."

"Then it's all yours," Wilkinson said, pushing the envelope to Gaby along with the paperwork she had given him earlier. "I don't know what else I can tell you. With no evidence of a crime, there was nothing more for the police to do. We filed the report, and I pretty much forgot about it until Matt here called."

"You've been very helpful, Detective Wilkinson. Thanks so much for spending the time with me. I really appreciate it," Gaby said, standing and shaking hands with Wilkinson once again, the paper-work and evidence envelope clutched in her left hand. "Just one more thing. Can you point me in the direction of the traffic division? I understand that I need a release to bring to Manhattan Impound so I can dispose of Jorgenson's truck."

"Matt knows the way. He can take you over," Wilkinson said, turning to Matt and patting him on the shoulder. "Hey, guy. Don't be a stranger."

"I'll be talking to you. Thanks for taking the time with us today," Matt responded, shaking Wilkinson's hand, then turning to lead Gaby down the corridor toward the traffic division.

Once Gaby had secured the release from the traffic division, a simple process since there were no unpaid traffic or parking viola-tions to be cleared, she slipped everything into her briefcase.

"I guess the next stop is Bellevue and the morgue," she said to Matt, who suggested they stop for lunch first.

"I know a deli over in that direction. It's a nice day. Mind a walk? It isn't that far."

# Chapter 21

THEY ENDED UP AT THE MOONSTRUCK DINER, AN OLD-TIME
eatery with typical retro décor. As they slid into an available booth,
they were greeted by a young busboy who filled their glasses with
water, picked up the extra cutlery and menus from the table, and said
that their waitress would be by in a few minutes.

It took them a while to get past the lengthy breakfast menu and on
to the equally lengthy lunch listings. There was little on the menu that
appealed to Gaby, so she chose what seemed like the most innocuous
item, a vegetarian wrap, while Matt ordered the Reuben "deluxe,"
which ended up being served with fries, coleslaw, a pickle, a limp leaf
of lettuce, a pale tomato slice, and what looked like a recycled red
onion ring. He had coffee, while she stuck with water.

"I hope the visit to the Ninth was helpful," Matt said after drown-
ing his fries in ketchup and taking a big bite of his Reuben.

"Very," Gaby answered. "Thanks again for setting it up. Detective
Wilkinson was able to give me a picture of what might have happened
to Jorgenson, which I hope I can confirm with the medical examiner.
Still not sure what he was doing in New York, but that seems like a
dead-end to me. I was really happy to get that envelope of personal
items, especially the keys. There's a room on a lower level of the house

that I haven't been able to get into. I'm hoping the key to that lock is on his key ring."

"Good. I was surprised when I learned it was Brad Wilkinson who caught the case. We go back a ways."

"Yeah. Seemed like you knew each other." Curious about the exchange that had taken place between Matt and Wilkinson, but reluctant to delve too deeply into unknown territory, Gaby asked, "Did you work together when you were in New York?"

"We were in the academy together, graduated at the same time, and were both assigned to the Ninth. I moved to the Bronx after I got married, and I put in for a transfer and worked from there. Haven't seen Brad for years."

They ate their sandwiches in silence for a while. Then Gaby asked, "How's your family adjusting to the move to Connecticut?"

Matt sat back, eyes narrowed, lips pursed, staring at the floor.

"Sorry! Did I say something wrong?"

"Julia. Her name was Julia." Matt glanced back up at her. His face softened. "She was just seven years old. Killed by a driver drunk or high on something. She was walking with her mother. Coming home from ballet lessons just a few blocks away."

"Oh, Matt... No! I'm so, so sorry."

"Her mother... Brenda... my wife. She was hit too. Died a few days later. She was pregnant with our son. She miscarried, bled out. The baby couldn't be saved." Matt's eyes glistened with unshed tears as he looked at Gaby. "Worse yet, they never caught the guy, so there wasn't even a sense of justice."

"How terribly sad."

"You just have to move on after something like that. The change of scene and pace in Connecticut was a help." Matt's expression softened even more. "Still have my moments, but you keep going. You have no other choice."

Gaby remained silent, looking at Matt through fresh eyes. Part of her wanted to share her own loss, but she held back. She didn't want to make her own encounter with unexplained violence and the loss of a spouse a "me too" story. She'd encountered too many similar tales from well-meaning students and colleagues after her own loss and had cringed at how unsupportive such sharing could be.

Matt signaled the waitress for the check.

"My turn," Gaby said, "please."

"Okay. How about I leave the tip." Matt looked at his watch. "Better be going. Maybe we'll be able to head back up to Woodson Falls before the evening rush hour."

"Good idea." She paid the bill at the cashier's station near the exit and, leaving the restaurant, they walked the few blocks to Bellevue in silence. The sunny day had suddenly turned cloudy and breezy.

"Looks like it might rain," Matt said as they approached the building. "Why don't I get you to the medical examiner's office then head back and get the car. I'll park in the garage and wait for you in the lobby.

"Sounds like a plan."

After showing their identification and indicating where they were headed, Matt and Gaby made their way to the morgue.

"Do you have your cell phone with you?" Matt asked.

"Sure, why?"

"Why don't I put my number in it so you can call me if you finish up before I'm back?"

"Okay. That'll work." Gaby handed him her phone. He entered his cell number, then gave it back.

"See you in a bit. Good luck."

"Thanks, Matt."

Matt left while Gaby gave her paperwork to the receptionist, then sat on the bench provided for visitors, waiting for someone from the medical examiner's office to come out to collect her.

After several minutes, Mr. Gallagher, who introduced himself as the senior caretaker of the morgue, showed Gaby into a small interior office furnished with a metal desk and chair, a filing cabinet and a straight-backed guest chair. The space seemed oddly cramped for someone who oversaw an operation as vast as the New York City morgue, which itself had been relegated to the basement of the sprawling Bellevue Hospital Center complex.

After looking over the documents appointing Gaby as the administrator of Jorgenson's estate and verifying her identification, Gallagher slipped on a pair of glasses and consulted his computer. After a series of taps on the keyboard, Gallagher glanced again at the death certificate. "Jorgenson, Jorgenson," he muttered as his fingers made their way over the keys. "Why is that name so familiar? Jorgenson."

"Ah, here we are," he said a few minutes later. "Jorgenson, Pieter. Arrived at the morgue on January 23rd. Hmm… This is unusual. The body was never autopsied. Dr. Garrity handled the case. Apparently, what history was gleaned from the police detective who accompanied the body to the morgue led Garrity to order a CT scan, which showed a burst aneurysm in the brain, consistent with the detective's report of a witness' statement about what he had observed. Since there was no evidence of trauma or illness, I guess Garrity decided to forego an autopsy. His prerogative."

Gallagher turned to Gaby and said, "No autopsy would mean the body could be offered to one of the city's medical schools. They're desperate for cadavers. Since no one had come forward within the time allowed for someone to claim the body, the record indicates that Jorgenson's body was sent to New York University's medical school back in February."

"What happens when the school is done with it? Would the body ever be released for burial?" Gaby asked.

"The school is required to return the body to the morgue. The usual next step is burial on Hart Island—New York's potter's field. In your case, assuming you're looking to have him buried in Connecticut, you'd have to contact a New York funeral home and make arrangements for them to transfer the body to a funeral home in Connecticut. We've used Gannon Funeral Home, which is close by. I'd recommend making arrangements with them." Gallagher handed her a business card with the contact information for the funeral home.

"When would that happen?" Gaby asked next, placing the card in her briefcase.

"Probably June at the earliest. Sometimes longer. End of the school year, usually, after some budding young surgeon or medico learned all he could through dissecting the body."

Gaby handed Gallagher her business card, and he entered her contact information into Jorgenson's file in the computer along with scans of the official documents she had provided.

"Thanks so much for your help," Gaby said, shaking Gallagher's hand and gathering her purse and briefcase, ready to exit the office.

"Ah, now I remember. We had a young man working here years ago when I first started. Name was Jorgenson. Wonder if it was the same person? Our Jorgenson worked as a janitor. Was fired after a few months. Too nosy about the morgue. Hung around a lot after his shift. We suspected him of trying to enter the morgue after hours. Creepy guy. Haven't thought about that for years," Gallagher said, shaking his head. "Nice to meet you, Ms. Quinn. We'll contact you when Jorgenson's body arrives back here."

Gaby made her way up to the hospital lobby and found Matt waiting for her there.

"Where next?" he asked, taking his car keys from his pocket.

"Last stop is Manhattan Impound, across town I'm afraid, at Thirty-Fourth Street and the West Side Highway."

"No problem. It's a relatively straight shot back to Connecticut from there."

As they made their way to the parking garage, Gaby said, "If it's okay with you, I'd like to take whatever's left in Jorgenson's truck back to Connecticut. According to Detective Wilkinson, it's quite a lot of stuff. Maybe it's a good thing you have a station wagon."

# Chapter 22

WHILE GABY AND MATT MADE THEIR WAY ACROSS TOWN IN stop-and-go traffic, heading toward the Manhattan Impound lot on the Westside, Gaby told Matt what she had learned during the trip.

"As luck would have it, I won't be able to reach my primary goal for coming to New York for quite a while. It'll be months before Jorgenson's body is returned to the morgue from the medical school at NYU."

"Will that delay you in settling his estate?" Matt asked.

"I've still got to empty the house and put it on the market. And then there's the legally required five-month period for creditors to make claims against estate assets, if there are any—claims that is—which I doubt. So, everything will probably be ready for settlement around the time I'm able to have Jorgenson's body buried next to his mother in Prescott's Evergreen Cemetery. At the very least, it's good to know I won't have to get his body exhumed first."

"I know getting Jorgenson's keys was important. What else?"

"Well, talking with Detective Wilkinson and then the morgue caretaker confirmed that Jorgenson died of natural causes, even though he was relatively young. That means I don't need to pursue a wrongful death claim. I don't think I'll ever know why he was in New York when he died. Still, since the police didn't pursue anything around the incident that might have indicated Jorgenson was involved in illegal activity or was the victim of a crime, the reason he was in New York seems pretty much irrelevant at this point."

"You sure do go down a lot of rabbit holes," Matt commented.

"Huh?"

"You *don't* have to exhume the body, there probably *aren't* any creditors, you *don't* need to file a wrongful death claim. Seems like there are as many 'don't have to's' as there are things to do."

Gaby laughed. "That's just the way the law works. It takes more than getting the right answer to succeed on law school exams. You need to put your intuition on hold for a while and, instead, go down every blind alley and discuss why each one doesn't lead to the right answer."

"Did you enjoy law school? I've sometimes thought of giving that a try."

"Actually, I did enjoy it. I liked the intellectual challenge, although sometimes it felt like I was sitting on a knife-edge."

It was Matt's turn to say, "Huh?"

"Thinking like a lawyer means being able to see both sides of an issue and argue each successfully. In theory, that allows the attorney on one side of a matter to predict an opposing attorney's arguments and be prepared to refute them. It's quite a brain tease, but I enjoyed learning to think that way."

"I guess that makes sense. And as for Jorgenson's estate, I can see how you'd want to rule out as much as you can along the way so there are no loose ends when you're finally able to close the matter."

"Exactly."

The wind had picked up significantly as they arrived at Manhattan Impound, the dark clouds racing across the sky. Gaby provided the officer manning the impound office with the necessary information to establish her authority to deal with the truck, along with the title to the vehicle, the release from the traffic division, and the cashier's check to cover the impound fees.

"I'd like to remove the personal items from the truck," she told the officer, "then ask that it be sold at auction if that's possible."

"Sure. We hold regular auctions of unclaimed vehicles and can include the truck in the next batch. The proceeds can be applied to any remaining fees and then sent to you as the executor of the estate."

"Great," said Gaby, relieved that this officer was much more amiable than the one she had spoken with on the phone.

"Who should the check be made payable to?"

"The Estate of Pieter Jorgenson. Here's my card. The check can be sent to my attention."

The officer recorded the information and had Gaby sign the title to the truck. "Truck's over in slot B49," he said, emerging from the office and pointing toward the right side of the lot. "Here's the key. Please lock up the vehicle and return the key to me when you're done."

"No problem, officer," Matt said. "We also expect to find some heavy articles in the truck. Mind if we bring my vehicle into the lot to off-load the truck?" he continued, showing the impound officer his police identification, which seemed to grease the skids.

Gaby walked over to where the truck was parked and unlocked the driver-side door while Matt brought the station wagon into the yard. She climbed inside the truck and began to remove the items in the glove box, placing them on the passenger seat along with the camera and map that were lying there. She got out of the truck when Matt pulled up.

"Maybe I can just pull the truck box out instead of off-loading its contents," Matt said, climbing into the truck bed and giving the box a heave. "Well, that's not going to work. Thing's bolted to the truck bed."

"Here are Jorgenson's keys," Gaby said, fishing them out of the evidence envelope. "Not sure which one will fit the truck box. I recall Detective Wilkinson saying his partner locked it up again after cataloging the contents."

Matt fiddled with the keys until the truck box opened.

"Could you hand me one of those plastic bags?" Gaby asked. "There's no room in the evidence envelope for the stuff in the glove box."

"Here you go," Matt offered. "I'm going to pull this large red carpenter's toolbox and the rest of the stuff to the tailgate so it's easier to move them to the wagon. After that's all packed, I'll grab whatever else is in the truck."

"Great," Gaby said, climbing into the truck cabin again and filling the plastic bag with the map, camera and glove box contents. "There's an open container with juices and snack packs of animal crackers behind the passenger seat."

"Got it," Matt confirmed, putting the box of juices and animal crackers in the wagon. "Guess that's it. We good to go?"

"I think so," Gaby replied, getting out of the truck and turning to close the door. "Oops. Looks like there's some garbage on the floor under the driver's seat. Can you hand me another plastic bag?"

She reached in to pull out two empty juice boxes and an animal cracker package that held some crumbs, tossing these into the bag Matt held out for her. "I'd better check the passenger side as well," she said, walking around the truck and opening up the door. "Nothing."

Matt knotted the bag and added it to the pile in the back of the station wagon.

"Now we're done," she said, climbing into Matt's wagon, "and just in time." Heavy drops of rain had started to fall as they left the impound lot. They dropped off the ignition key as well as the key to the truck box with the impound officer and headed to the highway.

Their ride back to Connecticut was uneventful, their pace outstripping the rain clouds. The slow-moving storm probably wouldn't reach Woodson Falls until later that night. As they approached Gaby's house, she turned to Matt.

"I can't thank you enough for setting up the meeting with Detective Wilkinson and for coming with me today. I could have made the trip on my own, but I don't think things would have gone as smoothly as they did if you hadn't been there. I still don't understand why you'd give up a day off to do this, but I am truly grateful you did."

"Really, Gaby, it was nothing. Besides, you told me you had planned to go into the city by train. How would you have handled securing all this stuff from the truck? Speaking of which, where do you want me to put it all?"

"Let me open the trunk to my car. You can put everything in there. That way I can take it all up to Lakeview Terrace the next time I'm at the house, hopefully, tomorrow," Gaby said, getting out of Matt's wagon and opening the trunk of her car for him and then the door to the house to let Kat out.

Matt moved the toolbox, duffel bag, plastic bags and the box of juices and cookies to Gaby's car. "What about this?" he asked, holding up the bag of garbage.

"Just toss it in with the rest. I'll end up ordering a dumpster when I finally get to emptying the house, and I'll get rid of it then." She reached into the wagon to retrieve her purse, briefcase, the evidence envelope, and the plastic bag containing the contents of the glove box.

"I'll be heading out then," Matt said, closing the Subaru trunk.

"Sure you wouldn't like to come in for a cup of tea or a glass of wine?" Gaby asked, feeling like she'd miss his company after their long day together.

"It'd be better if I got back to my place before it starts to rain. Maybe another time?"

"Sure," she answered, juggling the things she was carrying while she turned back to the house as Kat returned, wagging her tail. "Drive safely. And, Matt, thanks again."

# Chapter 23

THE SLOW-MOVING STORM THAT GABY AND MATT HAD MANAGED to stay ahead of as they drove back to Connecticut finally reached Woodson Falls later that evening. Gaby was working at her desk, catching up on mail and paying bills, when she was startled by the sudden flash of lightning outside her window, followed immediately by a booming clap of thunder that shook the cottage, loudly announcing the storm's arrival. The thunder set Kat to whimpering as she scurried under the desk, lying on Gaby's feet and shivering in anticipation of continued rolls of thunder that never arrived.

The torrent of rain that followed the thunder pounded on the cottage roof, continuing through the night and into the following day. When Kat came in after a brief visit to the woods in the morning, she was drenched. Gaby stood ready with a large towel to greet her before the dog christened everything in the room with a shake of her thick coat, which was heavy with rainwater.

Gaby had hoped for a better day to return to the house on Lakeview Terrace. While she wanted to bring the items that she and Matt had removed from the truck into Jorgenson's house or garage, that could wait. She was more interested in getting into the locked room to complete her exploration of the house and strategize an approach to emptying its contents in preparation for the sale of the property.

She just hoped one of the keys she'd gotten with Jorgenson's personal effects worked to open the door to the room.

When the storm lifted briefly later in the day, Gaby ventured out into the drizzle she hoped marked the storm's end. She stopped at Mike's Place to pick up a hot cocoa to bring with her to Lakeview Terrace.

"What a streak of weather we're having," she said to Mrs. Browning as she checked out.

"Yes indeed," the clerk replied. "My daughter-in-law Karen works at the post office, and she told me the carriers can't deliver mail to a lot of houses, especially up in the Estates. Between the rain we've been having, the high-water table, and snowmelt, the mud's so deep the dirt roads up there are impassable."

Gaby groaned inside at this delay in completing her work at the house, but was glad to have been spared the risk of getting mired down in the mud.

"Thanks for letting me know," she said. "I had planned to head up there. Maybe I'll have my cocoa here and take the opportunity to catch up with Emma," she added, turning back to the rear of the store.

"I'm sure she's free. This rain has kept everyone indoors. Except for the road crew, we haven't had many customers today."

It was pouring again by the time Gaby returned home. Frustrated at her inability to move ahead with the estate, she decided to call Lucas to let him know about the delay that would occur before his nephew could be buried and to find out whether he wanted anything from the house. Then she planned to review what she knew so far, hoping to fit together more pieces of the puzzle that was Pieter Jorgenson.

Lucas picked up on the first ring.

"Hello?"

"Hi, Mr. Jorgenson. It's Gabriella Quinn, the attorney working on your nephew's estate. How are you today?"

"I'm okay. Did you get to New York like you planned?"

"Yes, I did. I learned that Pieter's body had been donated to a medical school. His body should be released back to the morgue toward the end of June, or maybe a bit later. Then I can arrange for his remains to be transferred up to Connecticut for burial next to Sofia."

"Well, at least some good might come from him dead. Certainly didn't contribute anything to society while he was alive. And you said the cost of all that would be paid by the estate?"

"Yes. Actually, there's a fair amount of money in bank accounts and there'll be more when the house is sold. You could help me get the money to the right people if you could draw up a family tree showing your parents, your siblings and the children each had. The court will ask for that in determining the beneficiary or beneficiaries of the estate. Would you be able to do that for me?"

"Sure."

"It'd be really helpful if you could indicate when any of those people passed away as well."

"I can do that. Anything else?"

"I'm wondering if you want anything from Pieter's house."

"Can't think of what I'd want. My wife keeps bringing home junk from tag sales. Got so much useless stuff I can't park in the garage. Don't want to bring in more odds and ends we don't need."

"I understand. If I happen to come across something that might be of interest to your family, I'll let you know. Otherwise, I'll probably sell or donate most of the things in the house."

"That sounds fine. I'll mail that family tree to you in the next week or so."

"Thanks so much. You have a good day."

"You, too."

Gaby had brought the plastic bag containing the camera, map and glove box items into the house with her when Matt brought her home last evening. Now she retrieved the bag along with the evidence envelope and notes from her New York visit. She added to the pile several of the files into which she had sorted various documents she had found in her initial exploration of the Lakeview Terrace house. She took everything to the kitchen table where she'd be able to spread out the assortment of materials as she worked through them.

She began with Jorgenson's wallet, where she found his Connecticut driver's license, a training verification card from the Carpenters International Training Fund as well as an out-of-date membership card from the National Roofing Contractors Association. No health or dental insurance cards. Several school pictures of young girls were tucked into a pocket of the wallet, penciled names on the back of each suggesting the photos were of his cousins, Sonia, Sylvia and Brianna. Beyond those items and Attorney Paul Evans' business card, which the police had returned to the wallet, there was only some cash—$63 in twenties, tens and singles. She made a note to add the cash to a revised inventory for the court after she deposited it into the estate account.

She had pocketed Jorgenson's keys when she and Matt left the impound lot and retrieved them now to add to the pile on the table. Sorting through the keys, she felt for sure that one would open the door to the locked room on the house's lower level. She linked the set of keys Rusty had given her when he changed the locks at the Lakeview Terrace house to the keys from the evidence envelope and placed them in her purse so she'd be sure to have them when she was able to return to the house.

She emptied the plastic bag containing the items she'd found in the truck's glove box as well as the camera and map that had been left lying on the passenger seat. Nothing from the glove box was of much interest. The notebook contained some reminders of past appointments but no concrete information about who Jorgenson might have met with or where on the day he had died.

The camera was a simple Kodak PixPro digital model with a zoom lens. Since Gaby had found no evidence of a computer in the Lakeview Terrace house, she assumed Jorgenson had the pictures developed at Walmart or similar store offering such services, unless Jorgenson had an office with a computer and printer in the locked room. She scrolled through the pictures on the camera, which showed scenes similar to those depicted in the photos she had found in Jorgenson's dresser drawer.

The phone rang. "Law offices, Gabriella Quinn speaking."

"Hi, Gaby. It's Matt."

"Good morning, Matt... or is it afternoon. I've lost track."

"Still morning," he replied with a chuckle. "I'm glad I caught you. I figured you'd want to be going up to the house in the Estates and wanted to warn you off. I've spent most of the morning with the road crew trying to clear the roads up there from stranded drivers who swerved into a ditch or were mired down in the mud. It's really not safe to drive up there."

"Thanks for thinking of me. I was out earlier and found out about the road conditions before heading up there. Guess I saved myself a headache."

"Absolutely. I'd let things dry out for a few days after this rain stops and, even then, wait until the roads are re-graded and free of all the ruts made by spinning tires."

"Okay," she agreed reluctantly. "I'll check with the road crew before venturing up there."

"Or you could call me."

"Or I could call you," she replied, smiling to herself. "Thanks again for the warning."

"No problem. Enjoy the rest of your day."

"You, too. Bye, Matt."

Turning back to the pile of things on the kitchen table, Gaby opened the map she'd found on the front seat of the truck. Several areas were circled, mostly parks. There were faint pencil notations on some of these that were difficult to decipher. She went to her office desk and found a small magnifier and brought it back to the kitchen.

Only one of the circled locations in Manhattan carried a date and number: September 20 and the number 2. Of the smattering of circled locations in the Bronx, two carried dates and numbers: August 7 and the number 1 and November 15 and the number 4. Three locations in Brooklyn were circled; only one was dated—October 14 with the number 3. Several locations in Queens were circled. Again, only one was dated—December 12 with the number 5.

Intrigued, Gaby pulled out the calendar she had filed away with the rest of Jorgenson's papers. Flipping through the calendar pages, she discovered the dates and numbers on the map matched the notations on the calendar. And the initials noted on the calendar matched up with the boroughs on the map. She turned to the pile of pictures and, turning them over, matched these to the dates, borough locations and numbers. Jorgenson must have had a reason for such a systematic approach to these recordings, something important to him, but what it all meant remained a mystery to Gaby.

Shaking her head, she sorted through the files containing information relevant to the estate, coming at last to the one file that contained a curious collection of clippings that had no seeming relation to the estate. It was an odd and, in some ways, troubling assortment. She wasn't quite sure why she had bothered taking it from Jorgenson's filing cabinet.

Most of the clippings were health-related in one way or another, again suggesting Jorgenson had a fascination with all things medical. One clipping reported on the successful transfusion of blood from the dead, suggesting the technique might be useful in battle or a mass casualty event.

There was an advertisement selling a pattern for making a birdhouse. Perhaps that was what prompted Jorgenson to put his carpentry skills to work on this endeavor.

A small collection of articles related to nature was intriguing. One answered the question of whether worms had eyes (no, but they do have light-sensitive cells over most of their bodies that enable them to distinguish between dark and light). Another reported on a caterpillar that was proving a menace to oak trees. Jorgenson had dated the pieces, all a good twenty years old, which made Gaby wonder why he had retained them.

Several articles reported on a tear gas gun disguised as a pencil or pen, along with a tag written in what appeared to be Jorgenson's now-familiar handwriting reading, "William English, Tear Gas Gun. Captain Butt an expert fired a bullet from this gun on a vise and broke the gun. The test failed." She'd found no evidence that Jorgenson had the gun in his possession.

Most curious was a full-page cartoon titled "The World's Greatest Superheroes," depicting Batman, the Hulk and Superman locked in a glass cage within a laboratory built by the mad scientist, Surgeon Giles Manning. His apparent plan was to transplant his brain into a functioning body as a means of overcoming his own paralysis. Gaby laughed to herself at the thought that such a laboratory might be behind the locked door in the lower level of the Lakeview Terrace house, rather than a home office or, more likely, a bedroom, or possibly a washer and dryer unit.

As much as Gaby tried to consider these odds and ends from Jorgenson's house and truck objectively, as just odds and ends, she couldn't shake the feeling that something dreadful, possibly even sinister, was lurking just below the surface.

# Chapter 24

THE RELENTLESS RAIN LASTED FOR THREE MORE DAYS, HAMMER-ing on Gaby's roof and collecting in pools in areas where the ground remained frozen. The run-off from melting snow joined with the rain to swell the rivers and brooks that traversed Woodson Falls. Streaming from the lake, Woodson Brook overflowed its banks. North of Woodson Falls, the road to Appleton was submerged, impassable to traffic. A brisk breeze forced the storm to finally leave the area. A bright sun replaced the low, dark clouds and began to dry the soggy land.

Gaby and Kat took advantage of the sunshine to take a long run. Gaby's ankle had been aching with the arrival of the storm front, but seemed to have benefitted from the enforced rest.

The trees had begun to leaf out despite the persistent rain. Collected raindrops from the green canopy sprinkled down on them as they ran, but they didn't mind. The exertion was a welcome relief. Both had been irritable while being confined indoors for the past few days.

When they returned to the cottage, the light on Gaby's answering machine was blinking.

"It's me, Gaby. Matt. Matt Thomas. Just wanted to let you know the road crew has finished re-grading the roads up in the Estates, so you're free to go up there anytime. Let me know if you need me for anything. Have a great day."

Gaby smiled to herself. It was nice having someone care enough about her to pick up on her eagerness to return to Lakeview Terrace and offer to help her get there.

She grabbed a quick breakfast after feeding Kat and changed from her running clothes into jeans and a sweatshirt. She didn't look very "lawyerly," but tackling the work to be done at the Lakeview Terrace house promised to be dusty, if not downright grimy. Calling to Kat to join her, she hopped into her car and made her way through town and up to Woodson Lake Estates.

With no ice or snow to worry about, coupled with the recent re-grading of the roads, Gaby decided to take her car down the drive-way and into the breezeway between the garage and house entrance. She needed to unload the things she and Matt had removed from Jorgenson's truck while they were in New York, and the toolbox and other items were too heavy to carry down the steep driveway.

Turning into Jorgenson's driveway, she was halfway down the incline when she saw another car headed up the driveway from the adjoining house, past the jumble of cinder blocks that had once run along the property line. As she put her car into park and engaged the emergency brake, a man leaned his head out his window.

"I think you took a wrong turn, missy," he shouted to her. "Who are you, and what are you doing on this property?"

Exiting her Subaru and signaling to Kat to stay in the car, Gaby stood in front of the man's vehicle, further blocking his exit.

"My name is Gabriella Quinn. I'm an attorney. I've been appointed by the probate court to manage Pieter Jorgenson's estate," she responded. "And you?"

"I'm Jorgenson's next-door neighbor, Ralph Loomis. We watch out for our neighbors up here. Can't be too careful, you know. Now, I'm late for an appointment. Would you kindly back your car up so I can pass?"

"Just a few questions, Mr. Loomis," Gaby said, not moving. "What can you tell me about your neighbor, Mr. Jorgenson? I never met him."

"Big guy, nasty. Mostly kept to himself although I understand he liked to sue people. I got caught up in that too. My lawyer told me he died and that's why he didn't show up in court. Can't say I miss the guy."

"Anything else? Did you ever happen to meet his mother, Sofia Jorgenson?"

"Yeah. Saw her a few times. Sickly looking lady, but nice enough. Heard she passed away last year. My wife and I were in Florida at the time. Otherwise, we might have…"

"What else can you tell me about Mr. Jorgenson?"

"Came and went a lot, especially after his mother died. Kept odd hours. Always carrying stuff into the house, but not much out. Pretty heavy loads it seemed, by the looks of the bulky duffel bag he carried now and then, slung over his shoulder. Didn't want anyone to help out. Didn't like anyone asking questions." Loomis paused briefly then said, "Now can I pass?"

"You *do* understand that you're trespassing," Gaby responded.

"No, no. Got *that* wrong. I won in court, especially after Jorgenson was a no-show."

"What you won was the right to purchase an easement to pass over Pieter Jorgenson's property, and until you do… well, technically, you're trespassing. I do understand your situation here, and I'm willing to let it go for now. Is Bill Harrison still representing you?"

"Yeah. Know him?"

"I do. How about I work with him to resolve the easement issue?" Gaby walked up to the driver's side of Loomis' vehicle and stuck out her right hand. "Glad to meet you, Mr. Loomis. I'll be in and out of the house for the next week or so, getting it ready to put on the market. I'd like to get the easement issue settled before I try to sell the property."

"Okay, okay. Whatever. Gotta go. See ya," he said, giving Gaby's hand a perfunctory shake.

"Why don't you back up so I can pull into the breezeway? Then you can be on your way."

Loomis gave her a nasty look, then shifted his car into reverse, allowing Gaby enough space to squeeze through and into the breeze-way before he took off up the driveway.

Gaby pulled her car up far enough so as not to block Loomis' access to his house should he return before she was finished with her work today. She hoped she'd be gone before he came back. She wasn't eager to engage in another confrontation with the man, although she did want to emphasize the fact that he was trespassing on Jorgenson's lot.

"Stay, Kat," she said to the dog before popping the trunk. She unlocked the garage door then hauled in the toolbox, setting it on the workbench. She added the duffel bag and roll of plastic bags on the bench next to the toolbox. As she tossed the bag containing the empty juice boxes and cookie package into the garage, she recon-sidered leaving the roll of plastic bags there. She could use those to collect garbage from the house. Retrieving them, she relocked the garage door.

Opening the door of her car, she beckoned Kat to come out. She unlocked the house, letting Kat enter before she did, and put the roll of bags on the kitchen counter along with her purse and briefcase. She left the door open while she returned to the car to hoist the box of unopened juices and cookie packages onto her hip. She slammed the trunk lid closed, returned to the house, and put the box on the kitchen counter next to the bags, then relocked the door behind her.

The house smelled as if a small animal had gotten trapped inside and died. That stench dominated the musty odor she had come to expect, which seemed stronger than on her past visits. Still, the house had been closed up for so long that didn't seem unusual, especially with all the rain they had been experiencing and the house's loca-tion amidst the trees. She checked the windows and ceilings in each of the upstairs rooms but didn't see any evidence of leaks—or dead creatures. The vacant house insurance Gaby had secured would have covered any damage to the structure, but she certainly didn't want to have to deal with repairs or removing the remains of a dead raccoon or squirrel.

"Okay, Kat, let's go," she said as she approached the stairs to the lower level of the house and beckoned the dog to follow her. As she left the stairwell, she took a look around. Everything seemed to be just as she had left it, although the odor of decay seemed even stronger on this level. Keys in hand, Gaby headed toward the locked door, taking a deep breath before opening it with the one key she had yet to find a use for.

She stood in the open doorway, flipped on the light switch to the left, and gazed around the room. It was different than any other in the house.

"Stay close, Kat," she murmured, stepping in and looking around.

# Chapter 25

THE LARGE ROOM OCCUPIED ABOUT ONE-THIRD OF THIS LEVEL of the house. It gleamed in the bright light of the fluorescent fixtures retrofitted into the dropped white acoustical ceiling. The walls and floors were covered in white ceramic tile, a stark contrast to the rustic feel of the wood paneling in the rest of the house. Stainless steel cabinets with steel pulls had been installed below the ceiling along the wall to the right of the doorway. Between these and the cabinets and drawers below ran a metal counter interrupted by a deep sink.

"Why on earth did Jorgenson build this room?" Gaby stepped further into the space, Kat at her side.

In the far-left corner hung a life-sized skeleton. Gaby's body followed her eyes to take a closer look. Its presence in this sterile room almost seemed to hint at even more gruesome discoveries to come.

Beneath the skeleton was a wire basket that appeared to hold anatomical models, some of which Gaby recognized from visits to her orthopedic surgeon following the reconstruction of her ankle. Along the far wall, to the right of the skeleton, were a desk and swivel chair. Bookshelves were installed above the desk and held hardcover volumes of various sizes and colors. The titles focused on anatomy as well as forensic pathology, but most were guides for conducting an autopsy.

Her eyes were drawn from the books to the wall beneath the bookshelves. Pinned above the desk hung two charts printed on heavy paper. The charts were color depictions of male and female bodies with foldout layers that revealed frontal and rear views of the internal organs. Each layer of the charts showed a deeper level of the organs and their relation to one another and each organ was numbered to correspond with the numbers on accompanying charts listing each aspect of the body part being viewed.

With a shudder, Gaby recalled her conversation with the attendant at the Bellevue morgue. Was it possible that her Jorgenson was the same person who had worked there so many years ago? The same person who had shown an unusual interest in the bodies autopsied there? The books and autopsy manuals certainly pointed in that direction, as did the charts and that skeleton. Might this room be set up as an autopsy suite? But what could he possibly autopsy?

Knowing she would need to systematically catalogue the contents of this room as she had the other spaces in the house in the event there was something of value here, Gaby returned to the doorway and began a further exploration of the room with the gleaming cabinets and drawers along the wall to the right, starting with the upper cabinets and the drawers beneath the countertop.

A scale, calipers, a ruler and measuring tape were arrayed on a stainless-steel tray in the corner of the counter. Stacked in the cabinets were unopened boxes of disposable latex gloves, facemasks and slip-on shoe protectors along with numerous empty plastic water bottles and quart-sized Mason jars. Three of the drawers held open boxes of the gloves, facemasks and booties as well as several pairs of plastic protective eyeglasses. Others held scalpels, surgical clamps and retractors, forceps, scissors and boxes of suture materials and needles. Another drawer was devoted to several coils of plastic hosing with a brownish residue along the inner wall. The last drawer held what appeared to be surgical saws.

Now it was clear why there were medical supply catalogs in Jorgenson's mail. But why collect all these items? Certainly the right equipment for an operation or autopsy. But of what?

As she reached the far wall, Gaby made her way back toward the doorway, opening the lower cabinets as she went. She couldn't resist turning her head toward the corner of the room. She kept feeling the skeleton's empty eye sockets watching her every move.

Several gallon jars labeled "Formalin" were stored in one cabinet. More than a dozen of the plastic water bottles, filled with a dark brown substance, were in the next three cabinets. The final two lower cabinets held Mason jars with what appeared to be specimens of various body organs floating in fluid. Gaby recognized the specimens from leafing through the medical supply catalogs.

Were these animal or human organs? Could Jorgenson have been harvesting organs to sell on the black market? Yet storing these organs in formalin would negate that, so what else might they be for? And where did they come from? Did he purchase these specimens to feed his interest in medicine?

Overall, given the supplies stored in the cabinets and drawers and the tiled floor and walls, the room resembled a surgical suite, and Gaby thought back to the cartoon featuring Giles Manning's laboratory.

Two steel lockers were positioned against the left wall. Between these and the skeleton was a metal hospital gurney on wheels. On closer examination, the gurney seemed designed for something other than patient transport. There was no mattress. A shallow trough on each side of the gurney led to holes at the corners. Possibly for drainage? Is that what those hoses were for?

With trepidation, she opened one of the lockers. Hanging from hooks on the sides of the locker were white hospital gowns with tie closures, longer than the skimpy ones she had to wear when she was in the hospital. The second locker held several large, clear plastic bags containing child-sized shoes and sneakers. Neatly folded clothing lay on top of the shoes within each bag, which was knotted at the top and secured with strapping tape. She caught a glimpse of a belt buckle and tattered socks in one of the bags, but hesitated to open it just now. There was something familiar about the patterns on some of the clothes. She'd seen those patterns before and immediately thought of the dolls Jorgenson had carved and dressed.

Gaby hurried up the stairs to the main living area and picked up one of the smaller figures, turning it in her hand. The clothes on this figure seemed to be made from the same fabric she had seen downstairs, eerily similar to the match between the girl figure's dress and the clothes on the little girl seen in the photo taken at Bensonhurst Park.

Gaby headed back down the stairs to Jorgenson's secret room taking the doll with her to compare with the fabric she had spotted in one of the plastic bags. The fabric on the wooden figure of the boy was an exact match.

Placing the doll on the gurney next to the lockers, Gaby returned to the bookshelves. She had noticed five black-and-white marbled composition books along with the other books and manuals when she first peered at the shelves. It was time to see what they contained.

Gaby pulled down two of the composition books. The covers of both were labeled with the now-familiar notations of letters, date and number. Sensing the eyes of the skeleton on her, she pulled down the remaining three composition books and returned upstairs to examine them more closely, farther away from whatever had occurred in the room.

Pushing aside the birdhouse Jorgenson had been working on, Gaby sat at the worktable and opened the first notebook. Kat interrupted her, nudging her elbow, then dropping something at her feet. It was a teddy bear, smeared with mud.

"Kat!" Gaby exclaimed. "You can't do that!" She had brought the dog with her after the scare she'd had the last time she was at the Lakeview Terrace house. Now she was having second thoughts and considered taking Kat out to the car. The dog had never disturbed anything in other places Gaby had brought her. Why now? And how had the bear gotten so dirty?

"Were you outside?" But the front door was shut. Then where did the mud come from?

Grabbing the teddy bear and Kat's collar, she directed the dog into the bedroom where Gaby had seen the teddy bear on what she had assumed was Sofia Jorgenson's bed.

"Huh?"

Sitting on the bed, just where Gaby remembered it, was a teddy bear. *Then where did this one come from?*

Kat moved toward the bedroom door and whimpered, returned to Gaby, then walked back to the door, looking at her. It was clear that she wanted Gaby to follow.

"Hold on, Kat," she said gently. She suddenly felt compelled to open the two lower dresser drawers that had been blocked by the boxes of clippings. Positioned in orderly rows in each drawer were teddy bears identical to the one on the bed and the one Kat had brought to her.

Kat whimpered again and nipped gently at the sleeve of Gaby's sweatshirt, turning her head toward the door. It was a clear signal to Gaby that she should follow the dog.

"Okay, Kat. I'm coming."

Putting the muddy bear on top of the boxes of clippings, she followed the dog back into the stairwell. Kat whimpered again and directed Gaby down the stairs to the basement level.

A bare light bulb at the bottom of the staircase provided some light when Gaby flipped the switch on the wall before following Kat down the stairs, with more dim light coming from what Gaby assumed were basement windows.

Kat looked up at her, whimpering, when she neared the bottom of the staircase.

"Oh, my God!"

To the right of the stairs, partially revealed in a dirt floor that had been severely eroded by drainage seeping through the basement's cinder block walls, were five small child-sized graves. Visible through the dirt, resting in the arm of one of the partially decomposed bodies was a teddy bear.

# Chapter 26

GABY RAN UP THE BASEMENT STAIRS, KAT AT HER HEELS. HER hands were shaking as she quietly closed the basement door against the horror below before hurrying into Jorgenson's secret room. His laboratory? Autopsy suite?

"We've got to call Matt," she said to Kat. She turned off the lights and closed the door to the sterile room, leaving the key in the lock, before running upstairs to the main level.

She had anticipated her cell phone's "No Service" message, but clicked on her Contacts app to find Matt's cell number. The house's landline was still working. Gaby had kept up the monthly payments for the service, anticipating the possibility she might need to make a call or two sometime during her work on the estate.

Matt answered after a few rings. "Woodson Falls Resident State Trooper, Officer Thomas. Who's calling please?"

"It's me, Matt. Gaby. Can you meet me up at the Lakeview Terrace house? You need to see this."

"Are you okay? Should you call 911?"

"It's not an emergency, not really. But, but… you have to see this," she repeated, her voice trembling.

"Are you hurt? What's going on?"

"I'm okay. A bit shook up, but… Oh, Matt! I think I've discovered why Jorgenson was in New York. It's so awful. Graves. In the basement. Can you get here anytime soon?"

"I'm just finishing up with an MVA—a car accident—at the other end of town. I can be there in fifteen, twenty minutes. Is that okay?"

"Yes, yes. That's fine. It's number sixteen. Just—please come as soon as you can."

"Stay in the house and lock the door until I get there, okay?"

"Yes. I will. I'm safe. I have Kat with me. But… you need to see this."

"I'll be there as soon as I can."

Replacing the phone in its cradle, she turned to Kat, her eyes brimming with tears. The dog looked up at her, whimpering in response to her distress.

"Oh, Kat," she murmured, kneeling to hug the dog to her, the furry warmth easing the chill in her heart.

After snuggling with the dog for a few minutes, Gaby got up and went to Jorgenson's worktable where she had set the notebooks before calling Matt. She opened the notebook labeled "BX, 11/15, #4."

In Jorgenson's familiar handwriting, along with misspelled words, she read:

> SUMMERY OF SUBJECT
>
> Subject is male. Stated age is nine years. Taken from Van Cortlandt Park in Bronx, where he was watching some older boys playing basketball. Entered truck when offered a snack of cookies and juice.
>
> EXTERNAL EXAMINATION
>
> Subject is small for age, weighing approximatly fifty pounds. Under four feet tall. Appears to be severely malnurished.

> External inspection of the body reveels old
> bruises on torso as well as scarring on back
> and buddocks. Skin is intact but grimey. No
> hair in genital area or armpits; no facial hair
> growth noted.
>
> APPROACH
> A conventional Y-incision was performed
> running from sholders to sternum then
> continuing to pubic region with little resistance.
> Minimal subcutaneous fat noted.

The sophisticated language Jorgenson used to record his findings suggested he had lifted much of his wording from the many autopsy manuals Gaby had seen on the bookshelf downstairs.

The report continued on to detail the size and weight of the internal organs.

*Oh no! Those specimens I saw downstairs must have come from those poor children. And those water bottles… those must contain blood. Oh my God, were the children alive when he…?*

When she began reading Jorgenson's lengthy notations describing the procedure used to saw open the skull, Gaby closed the notebook.

Labeled "BK, 9/20, #2," the second notebook contained a report similar to the first, but beginning with an odd statement:

> Maybe this one will show me what make a kid
> the victum of a bully.

This child, also male, was approximately six years old. Jorgenson had found him sleeping in a doorway.

Were these homeless children? Runaways? They obviously had been alone when Jorgenson somehow convinced them to come with him. Had he lured each of them into his truck with the promise of a snack? A parent's worst nightmare… But where were the parents? Had they contacted the police? Were they still looking for these poor children?

Gaby heard Matt's car approach and opened the door with shaking hands as soon as she caught a glimpse of him leaving the patrol car.

"Oh, Matt! It's so awful."

"What is it? What do you mean 'graves?'" he asked, grasping her shoulders and looking at her intently.

"Downstairs—in the basement. Graves. Children," she replied, her eyes shimmering with tears.

"What? You've got to be kidding me. Show me."

"No! No! I can't, Matt. I won't. I couldn't bear going down there again. Seeing those…"

Giving her shoulder a squeeze, he said, "Then just tell me where to go."

Gaby led Matt to the doorway leading to the second floor.

"It's two flights down."

"Okay," he responded, pulling a large flashlight from his belt. "I'll be right back."

Several minutes later, Matt called up to Gaby. "I'm on the second level, outside the door with the key left in the lock. I'm guessing that's the locked room you wanted to get into?"

"Yes, that's it," she called down.

"Can you come down here? Just to this level, not the basement. I need you to show me what you found in this room."

"Okay," Gaby groaned, picking up the notebooks from the workbench and bringing them with her. "I'm on my way."

The trooper was standing in the doorway to Jorgenson's secret room when Gaby approached.

"Is this how you found this room?" he asked.

"Yes, except for these composition notebooks, which I took upstairs. I found them on the bookshelf there, above that desk. And the doll that's on the gurney. I brought that from upstairs." She quickly explained the connection she had found between the clothes on the carved doll and the fabric in one of the plastic bags of clothing stored in the locker as well as her assumptions regarding the little girl in the Bensonhurst Park photo.

"And other than those two things, nothing's been changed in this room?"

"No. I opened all the drawers and cabinets to catalogue the contents, but I didn't take anything out. Same with the lockers. I didn't move anything other than the notebooks." Looking up at Matt she added, "The notebooks have handwritten notes that look like autopsy reports. I think he was performing autopsies on those children. At least, that's the impression I got from the contents of this room and the entries in these notebooks."

"Gruesome. I can understand how shook up you must be. I'm feeling the same way myself. Let's head back upstairs. I've got to radio this into the Major Crimes Unit. They'll be taking over the investigation. Hang tight. I'll be right back."

It was awhile before Matt returned from the cruiser. Gaby was waiting at the front door, not wanting to take her eyes off the trooper. When he came back, he led Gaby toward the sofa at the end of the room.

"Let's sit down so I can brief you on what's going to be happening."

He cleared away the empty water bottles stacked on the sofa and chair. "Come. Sit with me.

"The detectives in the Major Crimes Unit will be taking over this investigation," he continued. "They're headquartered in Southbury, and they'll be coming out from there. They mobilize pretty quickly, but it still may be an hour or more before they get here. In the meantime, we'll need to sit tight and wait."

"Okay. I understand. What do you need from me?" Hearing the distress in Gaby's voice, Kat came over and put her head in Gaby's lap. She ruffled the dog's fur, the soothing action helping to lower her stress level.

"This house is a crime scene. After the Major Crimes detectives have interviewed you, you'll be free to leave."

"What? Will they think I'm a suspect?"

"I very much doubt that, but you'll need to explain your involvement with this and what you found."

"Okay. I can do that. At least, I think I can."

"Also, you probably won't be able to get back into the house until Major Crimes is done with their investigation. Judging from the scope of this crime scene—with so many bodies—of children—probably missing kids—the investigation is going to take a long, long time. I know you've been eager to move the estate issues along, but that may not be possible. Do you have enough to work with without needing to get back in here?"

"I'm pretty sure I do. Mostly it was that locked room that was left to deal with." Gaby looked down at her hands, which were shaking as she stroked Kat's head and back. "There's no way you'd ever get me to come back in here again—ever."

# Chapter 27

THE AIR WAS CRISP AND BREEZY AS GABY MADE HER WAY THROUGH the crowded parking lot to meet Nell Whitney for breakfast at the Sunshine Café. A quick burst of cold had turned summer's green leaves to brilliant reds, oranges and yellows. It promised to be a glorious fall. Even though it was early in the season, leaf-peepers from the city had been drawn to rural towns like Woodson Falls. Now they filled the restaurant for a bite to eat before taking in the spectacular display of foliage.

Nell waved to Gaby. She'd managed to grab a table for two near the door to the kitchen.

"Seemed like a good spot to catch up," Nell said, giving Gaby a quick hug. "We're not as likely to be overheard here."

"Oh, it's good to see you, Nell. It's been too long. Except for a few phone calls and our breakfast after I got back from the trip to New York, there doesn't seem to have been any time to get together."

"Well, you've been busy."

"Yes, indeed," Gaby responded. "All the publicity surrounding the Jorgenson case generated a good number of inquiries, along with quite a bit of law business."

"How's that going? The Jorgenson case I mean. Other than reports of the discovery of those children's bodies buried in the basement, the state police haven't released many details of the investigation."

"I think they're waiting until they're able to identify each of the victims. So far, only one has been tentatively matched to a missing child. The bodies were badly deteriorated and none of the children had dental work, so the police have had to use DNA and the children's clothing in an attempt to match them to people claiming to be their parents."

"You weren't considered a suspect, were you?" Nell asked.

"Matt—Officer Thomas, I mean. He told the detectives from Major Crimes how I had gotten involved with the case, and that I had discovered the graves and called him for help. They may have considered me as a possible suspect at first, but that was ruled out pretty quickly."

"That's good news, and a relief for you, I'm sure. Can you catch me up on what's been happening since you got back from New York? Have they involved you at all in the investigation?"

"A bit, at least at first," Gaby said, looking at the menu. Peggy was offering some intriguing, and tempting, October specials.

"I was able to match the letters and dates on the backs of the photos I showed you with notations on Jorgenson's calendar," she continued. "I pointed out to the detectives how both of these corresponded with notes on the map I found in Jorgenson's truck as well as with the notebooks he had used to enter the details of what he was doing. Once it was clear that Jorgenson had taken the children from New York to Connecticut, the FBI became involved."

"What can I get you, ladies?" Helen asked as she passed their table on the way to the kitchen. "It's a madhouse here, but I didn't want to keep you waiting too long."

"Those potato pancakes on the 'Specials' menu look pretty good to me," Gaby said.

"They're delicious and very popular. Bacon with that?" Helen asked with a smile.

"Not today. Actually, I think I'll try the sausages."

"Good choice. Sour cream or spiced applesauce?"

"The applesauce, please, Helen. And coffee when you can. Thanks."

"And for you, Ms. Whitney?"

"The same, I think. Sounds good. Coffee as well. Thank you," Nell answered.

After Helen had left the table, Nell asked, "How did the police ever figure out a possible identification for even one of the children?"

"Remember those photos I showed you?"

"Yes. You were trying to identify the locations where they were taken."

"Well, the photo you identified as having been taken at Bensonhurst Park—the one with the oddly named fish—had a little girl in it. Actually, it was that photo that gave me the first hint something strange was going on. The pattern on her dress seemed similar to the fabric used on one of the dolls Jorgenson carved."

"Was it?"

"Oh, yes. Once the police opened the plastic bags Jorgenson had stored in a locker in his 'workroom' and sorted through the contents, it was clear that each doll's clothing was cut from the clothing the children had been wearing. It seems that the dolls Jorgenson made were trophies and just might resemble each child he abducted. At least, that's what the use of the children's clothes on the dolls suggested."

"How awful! Back to my question, though. How did the police identify one of the victims?"

"The little girl's picture matched up with an Amber Alert that had been issued in Missouri several months ago."

"Missouri?"

"Turned out the child was a pawn in a custody battle. The father had taken her to New York, where he subsequently died of a drug overdose. The girl was living on the streets before Jorgenson came along."

"How awful!" Nell's eyes filled with tears.

"The entries in those notebooks he kept suggested Jorgenson's victims were lured into his truck by the offer of a snack."

"I guess I can see how that could happen, especially with a child who's alone and hungry. But how did he convince them to come with him to Connecticut?"

"We'll never know. Could be the children thought they were going on a vacation—or at least getting off the streets for a night. These were most likely runaways or homeless kids with few options. In any event, it turned out the juice boxes he offered as a snack along with packages of animal crackers were laced with a sedative. Matt was the one who noticed that the seals on the boxes we pulled from the truck had been tampered with—opened and then shut with a stick-on seal."

Nell smiled at Gaby's repeated use of the trooper's first name.

"There were some discarded juice boxes in Jorgenson's truck that I had put in a plastic bag while we were at the impound lot. I had tossed the bag with the empty juice boxes into Jorgenson's garage. They were tested at the lab, which confirmed the juice had been laced with a sedative, possibly left over from his mother's illness."

Helen arrived with their breakfasts and filled their coffee cups. "Anything else I can get you?" she asked.

"I think we're fine for now, Helen. Thank you," Gaby replied.

They paused in their conversation to eat.

"Mmm… These are delicious," Gaby said.

"Good choice," Nell replied, "but then it's hard to go wrong with Peggy's cooking."

After they had finished their meal and were sipping a second cup of coffee, Nell picked up their conversation.

"You seem to have an inside view of how the case is unfolding."

"Matt's told me a lot. He's been involved in the investigation, so he's been kept up on the details as the detectives put the case together. Of course, with Jorgenson's death, there's no one to prosecute, but there are sure to be wrongful death claims made against the estate by the parents of the victims—if more than that one little girl are ever identified."

"How gruesome. You haven't told me how you found the graves of those poor children."

"Actually, it was Kat who discovered them. Remember I told you this all started as a land dispute? The lots on Jorgenson's side of the road are all well below the level of the road. Jorgenson was worried about road drainage getting through the foundation and into his basement. He had refused to give his neighbor, Ralph Loomis, an easement to cross his property. Instead, he built a wall along his property line to divert the drainage away from his foundation. Loomis took the wall down after Jorgenson died. That terrible storm we had last spring, with all that rain, ended up eroding the dirt floor of Jorgenson's basement, partially revealing the graves."

"There was something about teddy bears in the latest newspaper account. I was surprised the police released that detail before the investigation was complete and they were sure they had their man," Nell said.

"They did hold back that detail until the evidence in the house clearly pointed to Jorgenson as the killer," Gaby responded.

"What were the teddy bears about?" Nell asked.

"Each of the children was buried with a teddy bear in their arms. Turned out there were a whole bunch of teddy bears in the drawers in Jorgenson's mother's bedroom. There were big boxes of magazine clippings blocking access to the drawers that I had Rusty move when I first got into the house, but I didn't open the drawers until Kat brought me the teddy bear from one of the children's graves. That's when I discovered the stockpile of bears Jorgenson apparently planned to bury with his future victims. The scariest thing we discovered was that there were children in Woodson Falls he'd given bears to as well. We can only imagine why. When Sally learned that Ryan had received one, she was beside herself."

"I hate to ask this, but were the children alive when Jorgenson worked on them?"

"Apparently not. Investigators found traces of DNA from the children on the inside surfaces of the plastic bags Jorgenson used to store the kids' clothing, as well as on the passenger seat of the truck, under a cushion Jorgenson had put on the seat. I missed that when I was at the impound lot and looking in the truck. Fortunately, the truck hadn't been auctioned off yet. The detectives' working theory is that at some point between New York City and Woodson Falls, Jorgenson put a plastic bag over the sleeping child's head, so the child suffocated and was dead when they arrived at the house. I remember Loomis mentioning Jorgenson carried heavy duffel bags into the house every now and then, but refused any help. The children might have been inside, already dead."

"It's hard to imagine someone doing that to innocent children. I guess we'll never know why," Nell commented.

"I know. I've thought a lot about it. The abductions began after Jorgenson's mother, Sofia, had died, so there may be some connection to his mother's death—like giving her the grandchildren she never had—but that's a stretch. There was no evidence of sexual abuse, but you've got to wonder, since he gave untainted packages of animal crackers to local kids as well, like he was grooming them for later or something."

"Indeed."

"There was a note in one of the composition books about discovering why certain children were picked on. Jorgenson's victims might have seemed to him to be victims of bullying. I remember his uncle mentioning Jorgenson was bullied as a child. I keep thinking back to a cartoon I found among Jorgenson's clippings that featured a mad scientist. Surgeon Giles Manning wanted to transplant his brain into a superhero. It's less of a stretch to think that Jorgenson wanted to find something in a child's blood or organs that could be 'fixed' to make the child less susceptible to bullying. Still, we'll never really know what was in his mind."

As they left the restaurant, Nell commented, "You'll probably have trouble selling that house once the police have released it as a crime scene."

"That's the funniest thing. I approached Loomis about the ease-ment issue. I had come up with a fair price for the privilege of crossing Jorgenson's property to get to the road. I wanted to tie up that loose end before the property went on the market."

"And?"

"Loomis said he wanted to buy the place so he could tear it down. Turned out the house blocked his view of the lake, and he was willing to pay to get rid of it."

# Epilogue

*(One Year Later)*

IT WAS LATE SUMMER BEFORE GABY HEARD FROM THE NEW YORK Medical Examiner's Office regarding the release of Jorgenson's body for burial. She had immediately called his uncle, Lucas Jorgenson, to determine the family's wishes in terms of a funeral. Lucas had wanted nothing to do with the matter.

"He can burn in hell for what he did to those poor children," he'd said before slamming down the phone. Lucas hadn't even asked about a possible inheritance. Connecticut law would have identified him as the beneficiary of Jorgenson's estate, but all the estate funds were being held in escrow pending the anticipated wrongful death suits by the parents of the dead children, if they were ever identified. No amount of money could compensate for the loss of a child, but that's what the law provided in a case like this.

Because cremation was the option with the least cost to the estate, Gaby had requested that Jorgenson's body be released to the Gannon Funeral Home in New York for cremation, with the cremains sent to the Wallace Funeral Home in Prescott for burial.

Now she stood on a knoll in Prescott Cemetery overlooking Sofia Jorgenson's grave. It was ironic, Gaby thought, that with his body donated to the medical school at New York University, Jorgenson had undergone the same procedures he had inflicted on the children he had abducted and killed.

Sofia's grave had been opened to receive her son's remains. There would be no service. Except for the funeral home staff, Gaby was the only witness to the burial of a serial killer.

Thank you for reading *Woodson Falls: 16 Lakeview Terrace*.
If you've enjoyed reading this book, please leave a review on your
favorite review site. It helps me reach more readers who may enjoy
the *Woodson Falls* series.

Subscribe to my newsletter at emeraldlakebooks.com/gabyquinn
to be notified when *Woodson Falls: 9 Donovan's Way*,
the next book in *The Gaby Quinn Mystery* series, is released.

# Author's Note

DID YOU EVER HAVE AN EXPERIENCE THAT LEFT YOU WITH THE uneasy feeling that there was more under the surface than you were able to uncover? *Woodson Falls: 16 Lakeview Terrace* was born from such an experience, one I encountered early in my law practice while I was working on the estate of someone I'd never met. It was a feeling that never left me even though the final resolution of that estate was nothing like the story you've been reading.

Shaping that uneasy feeling into a work of fiction was driven by my late husband's creative verve. John had a unique capacity to transform the everyday into an exciting fictional tale, a talent he applied as a paraprofessional at the Sherman School with his ongoing saga of the adventures of Leppy, our resident leprechaun.

*Woodson Falls: 16 Lakeview Terrace* is a work of fiction. While the story is drawn in part from my experience as an attorney specializing in estate planning and probate issues, it is my long service as the chief elected official of a small town in Connecticut that provides the story's color. My experience in office, most especially as a member of the board of a municipal insurance cooperative, underscored the reality that small towns share many commonalities, often invisible to the casual observer. The only real-life character in this book is Mr. Terrence Gallagher, who was senior caretaker of the morgue at Bellevue Hospital Center at the time the *New York Times* exposé was published. While the New York locations exist as described, the Connecticut locations depicted in the novel are fictional.

I am indebted to the members of Word Weavers Berkshires, a writing critique group, whose members helped to shape the story as it was being written.

I am particularly indebted to Tara R. Alemany, founder of Emerald Lakes Books, whose enthusiasm for the story coupled with her wisdom and guidance in molding it into the book in your hands were invaluable. The creative insight of Mark Gerber, Tara's partner and artistic force at Emerald Lake Books, was very much appreciated.

I am equally grateful to my first readers: James Early, Terri Hahn, Joseph Keneally, Susanna Marker, Eileen O'Connell, Daria Romankow, and Karen Tyler. Their input strengthened the writing and their enthusiasm for the story erased any lingering self-doubt.

Special shout-outs are due to former New Jersey District Attorney Ted Romankow, who fact-checked my legal references; Margaret Cook, who told me how a dog would signal its owner to follow; and Tim Alemany, who ensured the damage to Gaby's weathered Subaru was properly depicted and repaired.

It's my hope that you have enjoyed escaping into the world I've created in *Woodson Falls: 16 Lakeview Terrace*, and that you feel you could visit Woodson Falls and drop in for a meal at the Sunshine Café.

I invite you to join Gaby Quinn on her future adventures as she explores what lurks just beneath the surface of idyllic Woodson Falls.

# About the Author

H AVING RECEIVED A LIBRARY CARD BEFORE she began kindergarten (requiring her cursive signature), Andrea O'Connor began her writing career at the age of five with a short story describing the seasons. Her next endeavor, at age nine, was a novella featuring Christine O'Leary. So began Andrea's long love affair with the written word.

Singularly focused on a nursing career, Andrea continued to write for pleasure throughout high school and college. After completing a master's degree to teach nursing, she was offered a position as a nurse editor with the *American Journal of Nursing*, where she honed her writing skills through editing others' works.

Andrea was in the midst of writing a novel styled as a memoir when her husband John's Parkinson's disease progressed to the point where he was unable to engage in his usual active lifestyle. He longed to "do something," so she suggested they write a book together. She had long considered writing a mystery series based on some of her experiences in her second career as an attorney, and they settled on one of her early cases as the basis for a book.

It was a great opportunity for both. Andrea had left a long career in a "publish or perish" university setting prior to becoming an attorney. It was hard for her not to view writing fiction as lying on paper. John helped her to push the uneasy feeling that was the seed for *Woodson Falls: 16 Lakeview Terrace* into a believable plotline. Yet it was Andrea's long service as the chief elected official of a small town in Connecticut that provided the story's sense of place.

Andrea is the author of three award-winning texts in the area of nursing education and staff development as well as numerous articles in peer-reviewed nursing and education journals. *Woodson Falls: 16 Lakeview Terrace* is her first foray into the world of fiction, but it won't be her last. She collects teddy bears and birdhouses, loves to garden and bake bread, and writes from Sherman, Connecticut.

If you're interested in having Andrea come speak to your group or organization about this book or about the writing process, either online or in person, you can contact her at emeraldlakebooks.com/oconnor.

For more great books, please visit us at
emeraldlakebooks.com.

EMERALD LAKE
BOOKS
Sherman, Connecticut